Red Mist

By Andrew D Kimbell

Text Copyright © Andrew Kimbell 2018

First Published 2018

ISBN 978 198106 719 0

ALL THE BEST ROY

List of Plates

Chapter 1

Red Mist

In the Beginning

My name is William Henry Bennett, I was born in 1955 in Guildford, Surrey, and lived near the quaint little village of Peaslake in my parents' vast house, Burrows Cross. It was a huge mansion built in the last century and later partitioned into four separate homes, each one with at least five bedrooms. I grew up, like most children of that time and place, looking forward to the end of every school day so I could go out into the gardens or the woods surrounding that part of the county and get lost building dens and beating off unknown quantities of imaginary bandits, always immerging victorious and for the thousandth time declaring myself lord of the wood and defender of my little part of this wonderful country. Also, like all of my generation we grew up in a world that was still licking the wounds left over from World War Two. Of course, Surrey had been relatively untouched by the war but on rare occasions when I could come up with good enough excuses to be away for hours, I used to walk over the hills looking for war-related artefacts, spending hours searching and most of the time coming back with nothing but every so often I got lucky and I knew every aircraft crash site for miles and would always comb those areas with particular care. Because of this my room far out on the west wing of Burrows Cross closely resembled a museum. Bent pieces of metal, bullet casings, wartime uniforms and model aircraft adorned every wall.

Although countries of origin rarely came into my childhood dreams of bandits I was fighting bravely in the woods, if they did, they were often German, but when they weren't German they were American. Now to an outside observer this might have appeared strange as the Japanese would, in most children's minds at the time, been second in the line of evil and if I had been asked at the time, why Americans? I would have probably given some innocent or even defiant answer like "They just are," and in reality, I probably didn't really know why. Now, I do.

My parents' generation who had lived and fought through the war had done a wonderful job of patching up the physical damage done by it but in my family from a very young age I knew that the damage the war had done to hearts and minds was as severe and unrepaired to some in the fifties and sixties as it ever had been. Despite this, I had of course grown up hearing about the positive sides to the war from my friends in school and even the teachers and parents of friends. Great stories of daring doo's jam-packed with heroism, guns, bullets, and killing of the enemy for King and Country. But one place these stories never came from was my father. During those early years of my life I knew very little of my father's part in the war. In fact, I can sum up all I knew in a few brief lines. He had been in the Air Force as a pilot, he had been very brave, and he had been badly hurt, and that was about it. Although most children had never seen the darker side of war in those idyllic times, I was confronted with it every day. My father's face was very badly disfigured. Although the left side of his face was pretty much as it should be, the right side was, well, gone; burnt away by some terrible thing I was not allowed to know about. Now you may have thought that I would have found my father's face frightening but I didn't. To me, he was just my dad. Strict yes, quiet yes and of course he was frightening in all the ways a father can be when he's angry or when I knew I'd done something naughty and was dreading the time when he was going to find out. But his face to me was just a part of him. Deep down though there was a dark side to my father; so much he didn't talk about, so much he *would* never talk about and the fact he had few friends and no family. Where were my grandparents? Well that I was not to know for many years. Then there was the screaming. Bad enough as a child alone in bed at night in a big creaking old house trying to fend off the fears of darkness and the imaginary noises that weren't really there. Well, for me they were there; deep booming yells of terror and despair dwindling away to moans and sobbing as my mother was able to shake my father out of his nightmares and calm him down, wiping the sweat off his brow. But when taken as a whole, I remember my father as an all-round good father and in those rare moments where I and my father would joke, we occasionally made light of his injuries by laughing at the fact that he used to dribble down one side of his face when he ate. Of course, as the years passed I often tried to press him for information in my own way to try and learn something of my father's story, but I never found out anything. The only things I knew were the little I have already talked about and snippets of things dad used to shout in his nightmares: "Fire... Fire... get out boys, for God's sake... out... out... out... too low... too late," and often, "I told you, damn you, damn you all I told you." Finally, there was a name, always the same name. Tom, always Tom. On one breakfast after a particularly long night I asked my father who Tom was. The subsequent tirade ensured I never asked again.

In addition to these limited sources of information of course, like all children I picked up snippets of enlightenment from conversations overheard. I determined that there was at that time or had been a problem between my grandparents on one or the other side, and my parents, that my father had a deep-seated hate of politics and deduced that he seemed to have no love for the country for which he had lost so much and even less for the royal family who ruled it, but nothing, nothing matched his hatred of all things American.

My mother was a short, slender lady, almost as secretive as my father and like him she was the quiet type. She was from Devonshire and spoke with a very strong Devonshire accent like me, an accent my English teachers tried at great length and in vain to get out of me. I knew her parents lived in Torquay but I never met them. She spent most of her days cleaning the house. Cooking was one of her great joys, and, like me, she used to spend long periods wandering the gardens and in the summer helped Earl out with the weeding. Earl was our gardener. He was a tough old bull of a man, also from Devonshire, and an old soldier from the First World War. He had worked with my father in the Air Force during the Second World War but despite having lived almost his entire life far from his real home, his Devonshire accent was as thick then as it must have been when he first learnt to talk. I had long realised that Earl too, must have been sworn to the same secrecy as my mother however, for though he was fond of me, he never used to tell me a thing about his times with my father, no matter how hard I pushed.

Of course, all these little bits of knowledge and influence left me with a fascination for all things Air Force, and when I was not reading my school books I was going through books borrowed from the library in Shere, learning all I could. If I was really lucky my father would occasionally give me a book from his office about aircraft or the Air Force. I guess he thought that general knowledge of the Air Force was no bad thing and would do his secrets no harm. Also, of course, my parents were only too pleased that I was taking it upon myself to increase my skills in reading. My reading at that time was not fantastic but it was good enough, and anyway it was the pictures I was really interested in. I was blessed with a vivid imagination and it needed input.

One thing that did mark our family out from the average at that time was that neither of my parents worked. The house and gardens were huge, especially to somebody as small as me, money was never a problem, although both my parents were sparing with it, we always had everything we needed and we had a television, a telephone, a car and many other things I won't bore you with.

My world changed on the eleventh of February 1966. I had been away on a relatively short walk for me; short because it was bitterly cold, and as was generally the case in those days, I had found nothing of interest. When I walked through the garden and into the house I noted that the car wasn't in the driveway and wondered where my father had gone but I didn't give it much thought. I would have gone to my room to do some reading but I heard sobbing noises coming from the drawing room and went in. My mother was sat in a chair sobbing like her heart would break, her red face had tears streaming down it and I realised she had been in this state for some time. On seeing me she stood up quickly, wiped her eyes with her hanky and tried to smile. "Oh William, come and sit down, I have something to tell you." I didn't move. I knew my mother, she was my father's rock, and there was no reason on earth she would cry, save one. I knew what had happened before she even opened her mouth. How many times had I heard her reproach my father for driving the way he did or for having to buy another car when he had irreparably damaged the last?

My father's funeral was a day I have surprisingly little memory of. It was held at the little Peaslake church which was situated on a very steep hill at the top of which was the graveyard well-hidden amongst the trees of my beloved wood in which I had spent so much of my life playing. I remember sitting in the church with my mother on my right and Earl on my left. I remember tears, a lot of them, both mine and my mother's; even Earl was obviously deeply affected by the scene. The church contained about twenty people, some I knew, some I didn't. One person who did catch my eye was sat at the back. He was short and unmistakably foreign, either Chinese of Japanese I guessed. Who was this man? What could he possibly know of my father? These questions were questions for another day. After the short service, none of which I remember, my father's coffin was raised and with considerable effort, taken up the hill where it and he were lowered into the ground. Gone... and not to return. Very shortly after, Earl took my arm and I was walked home. My mother did not come with us. I remember as I walked away with Earl she stood a little away from the grave surrounded by a small group of men, one of which was the strange foreigner.

Chapter 2

More Questions Than Answers

The void in my life left by the death of my father was immense. In my mind the house grew ever bigger, colder and emptier than it ever had been. In the back of my mind was a deep sense of disappointment that I would never get to talk to my father about who he really was, what he had done, where he had come from. I knew that one day I would know most of these things anyway but I wanted to hear about these things from him, not from anybody else. I cried myself to sleep at night. Every fibre of my being screamed out silently. I wanted my daddy back.

My mother very quickly returned to her calm composure but it was obvious she was heartbroken. They had been married in 1954, when dad was thirty-five and had been inseparable ever since, according to Earl.

As I adjusted to the new way of things I found myself feeling slightly bolder than I had been in the past. It wasn't because, as Earl put it, I was now man of the house; I guess it was just with the passing of my father I had gone from being curious about my father's life before, to being tormented by a need to understand my father better than I did. This newfound boldness initially took the form of asking more questions to which I got the usual answers with a little more of the "He was a very good and brave man" from my mother than I had before. But as the weeks went by my mother began to go out on ever longer walks which increasingly left me alone in the house, and it was on one such occasion I found myself standing outside my father's office eying up the door. It was not locked, it never had been. There was an unwritten rule in the house that when father was in there he wanted to be left alone. I was forbidden to go in there and never had. I stood there for some time, whilst thoughts flashed through my mind. Mother's not here... she will not be back for some time... Earl's not in until tomorrow... father is... well... not here either... I am desperate to know more about my father's life... some, if not all, of the answers I seek are behind that unlocked door. Now today I have no doubt that God forbid the situation had ever been the same, my son would have been straight through the door but in my case, there was some invisible fear holding me back.

The heavy handle creaked as I turned it, as did the door as it slowly swung on its hinges and I stepped into a world I had not ever seen before. In the far-left corner of the room and under the heavy curtains covering the window and most of the light was a large dark wood desk with a dark green leather top. On it were some framed pictures, some pens, a lot of papers and mounted on a stand and made of solid brass was an aircraft. I'd have known that shape anywhere, it was a Spitfire, one of the late types. The walls were lined with shelves and on these were books in their hundreds, some of which I recognised as ones my father had let me borrow. On the left wall was a small fireplace with the various tools you associate with a fireplace spread out before it, along with some logs. As I looked round behind the door I saw a huge tough leather covered chest. The chest was not old but it had seen some serious experiences. Every one of the surfaces were either scratched or showed evidence of maltreatment. Dark circles on the lid showed where many a wet tea or coffee cup had been resting. And on the front of the chest was not one but two heavy locks which looked completely impassable. On the end of the chest that I could see were a few of what looked like symbols strung out in lines; I didn't have a clue what they meant. Only one wall of the office had been spared the bookshelves and that was the one to my right, and on this, photographs in frames a variety of sizes hung in a haphazard manner.

Taking in the scene I stared around the little dark room. One thought was uppermost in my mind... touch nothing! This learning process would need to be taken in stages. I walked forward making a thud, thud noise on the hard plank floor. I walked up to the desk and looked at the photographs. The first was a picture of me taken a few years ago. The second was of my mother, taken around the same time. The third was of a group of men standing under a two-engined aircraft I didn't recognise. Whilst I didn't know the aircraft I certainly knew the uniforms and flight gear; three of the men were pilots and the others were a combination of observers, navigators, wireless operators and so on. They were all dressed in shorts and short sleeved shirts with flying gear on top. Everything around the crews suggested desert. I leaned closer, yes, one of the pilots was my father. He had an arm round one of the crewmen and all were smiling from ear to ear. I had never seen my father with a smile like that, but most striking to me was that I had never seen him with two sides of his face the same. I stared, that face had been gone a long time, never to return. I dragged my eyes away and looked at the fourth picture. It was faded and showed a strange landscape. Snow-covered hills and some shabby what looked like outbuildings also covered in snow in the background and in the foreground about four or five single-engined aircraft in two lines. The aircraft had covers over them and snow over the covers. They were not spitfires. Far too big. Though not properly in focus, the large propellers, heavy landing gear and general shape as far as I could see it told me the aircraft were either Typhoons or Tempests. No, not Typhoons, no guns sticking out the front of the wings. These were Hawker Tempests. The picture must have been some place in France, or maybe Germany; there were no mountains like that that I knew of in England, maybe in Scotland but I doubted it. Turning to the brass model I gave it a glance and started to pay more attention to its elaborate stand. There were words here, no, not words, numbers and letters engraved into the brass. They read 127 SQN. Not fully appreciating the significance of what I was seeing and overwhelmed with excitement, I turned to the right wall. More photographs. The largest was another group photo but this one yielded more information. These men were all pilots and underneath each pilot was a series of names. There he was again, my father the only one without a name written under him, only now he was more recognisable. Although most of the men were smiling, my father was not and the damage to his face had returned, only even worse than I had ever seen it. The names were as follows:

FL Joe Price
FL John Fitzsimmons DFC
OL Herman Metzger
PO John Quinn
PO Tim Fitzsimmons
PO Hector Sharpe
FS George Kilmartin

I scanned the list again, then the photograph. FL (Flight Lieutenant), PO (Pilot Officer), and FS (Flight Sergeant) were all ranks I knew but OL was not one I had heard of and there was no way that a name like Herman Metzger was English, that had to be German. What on earth was Father doing flying with a German? This photograph must have been taken after the war? I moved on. There were many pictures of scenery and some of buildings. Another caught my eye. This was a picture of a ploughed field; it looked like one you might see just down the road, almost definitely England. In the centre of the field was a pile of twisted metal ablaze. I knew what it was, or rather what it had been, an aircraft, this was a crash site. Directly below that was another crash site scene but this one looked especially interesting because sticking out of the wreckage was the tip of a wing and on it was the unmistakable symbol of the United States Air Force. Unlike the first picture, this was no field, this was a hillside, a hillside covered in the same thick snow as in the picture on the desk. The final picture I looked at was of the back section of an aircraft I didn't recognise but taking up most of the picture was a top gun turret with a face starring out through the Perspex. That was a face I had seen before. I looked back to the desk. Yes, the man in the turret was the same man that my father had his arm around in the group photo on the desk. But there was more. Along the bottom of the photograph was written Canrobert 1942. I had no idea where Canrobert was and so moved on.

At this point my nerve was failing me, I should be getting out of here. Oh, hell I'm learning too much. My eyes were directed to the bookshelves. Good Lord, if I ever got the chance to go through that lot I would be the world's authority on every air force there had ever been, surely. Then my eyes fell upon a set of large books, no, not books, these were albums, photograph albums. My heartbeat went in to overdrive. In those pages I knew would be the answers to so many questions but they were on the top shelf and out of my reach. Not only that, but it was a step further than my nerve, at least for the time being, would allow me to go, so I turned and walked over to the trunk. There was no doubt, get in there and all secrets of my family would fade away but there was no chance. The only way of getting in there was to have Mother open it and there was precious little chance of that! It was time to leave.

A few weeks passed, maybe it was a month. I can't remember and my thirst for information only grew. I didn't know it at the time, but my window of opportunity was closing fast. I only visited the office one more time and learned little more as I was still too scared to touch anything knowing full well that my mother would notice. I would have returned but one day I came home to find a newly installed lock on the office door, I was horrified. Now there was no other way, I would have to wait.

Chapter 3

Upheaval

A few years went by and not long before my fifteenth birthday my mother told me that she felt we ought to move out of our house. My initial fears about the thought were quickly quelled when she announced that she had seen that a little cottage only about three hundred yards down the road was now for sale. I felt no particular connection to Burrows Cross, it was the fear of leaving the area that most worried me so on hearing we weren't, I agreed that it was probably for the best. I knew the cottage where she meant well, it was down Lee Hollow, just up from Jessies Farm and had once been home to the local farms overseer but he had long gone now. The house stood within a small walled garden but I didn't mind that, I still had all of the Surrey hills and though I would no longer have the commanding view from Burrows Cross on the top of the hill any more, somehow the cottage buried in the valley seemed cosier and isolated, and I liked isolation. Anyway, I'm wandering off. Despite the passage of time the interest in finding out more about my father had not diminished, if anything it had increased, but I had no way of getting into that office and any time I asked about it I was always greeted with a stone cold silence. It was frustrating in the extreme.

With the move came fresh thoughts of my father and one evening, sat in front of the fire with mother watching the television, I plucked up all my courage and determined I would have an answer I asked.

"Mother, when are you going to tell me about Father?"

With her eyes still on the television she replied, "Tell you what, dear?"

"You know what."

Now she turned and looked at me and every part of her face had changed from relaxation to severity, or was it fear?

I continued, "Mother, when we move, we will be taking all Father's things with us. I'm going to see them sooner or later, and I want to know about what happened to Father, what happened to the rest of our family."

Mother looked at me in silence, after what felt like an age she said, "William, when we move I will have your father's things packed up and stored, you are not ready to hear your father's story. But there will come a time, I promise you."

"Mother, I'm not a child any more. I'm almost fifteen. I've lost a father I barely knew anything about and I miss him, I miss him so much, at least if I knew about who he really was I might be able to... I don't know..." words failed me.

There was another long pause; though her facial features didn't change a single tear rolled down her cheek, then another down the other. Something of my determination must have communicated itself and she leaned forward and switched off the television.

"Alright, William, I will give it some thought and sort some things out for you to see. We will take it from there."

Amazed at how quickly she had relented after so many years of hitting a brick wall I said, "Thank you, Mother."

"I do have a condition though."

I waited.

"Your father's life was a complicated one and there were many sides to him, some you know about and some you don't. When you start to learn your father's story always keep a few things in mind. He was always a good man... always. But unfortunately, neither his family nor mine could see that. He made mistakes, we all do, but always know that he loved us very much even if he sometimes didn't show it."

"I will remember," I said, as if the conversation was over.

"I'm not done yet," Mother said, her voice had become stiff.

I stared at her again.

"Your father's story has been kept from you and others for good reasons. I have seen how badly you have always wanted to know about him, but all the time he was alive that was impossible, now he is gone." She paused and wiped her wet cheeks with her ever ready hanky. "Now he is gone. I suppose he is beyond harm, but we are not. Nothing... nothing of what you will learn is to be repeated to anybody, not your best friends, not to anybody, do you understand?"

"I do, Mother."

"Only Earl knows your father's story in detail and he would discuss it with nobody as he stands to lose just as much as you father would, were the story to be known."

"I understand. I will tell nobody, and thank you, Mother."

"Off you go to bed, William."

In bed I may have been but sleep, no chance. My head was a sea of unanswered questions, from the little Mother had said, it sounded like my father's story was complicated in the extreme but more than that, it seemed as though my father may have done something secret? Maybe something bad? And where did Earl fit in to all this? Finally, I fell into a troubled sleep.

A few weeks later the move began, most of the physical moving was done by a company Mother had paid to do the job.

Besides my father's office the only other place I had never been was the loft, well actually, that's not entirely true, I had been up there a few times and remembered it as a huge space covered in cobwebs with a single light hanging from the roof which shed a pathetic light through the area and throwing every corner, nook, and cranny into impenetrable darkness. What I had never seen was what was under them as everything was covered by thick dust sheets and I was not allowed to look. However, the ban had been lifted and so too were the sheets. Mother had pre-arranged that all artefacts and paperwork appertaining to the life of my father had been moved into his office and the office locked. Responsibility for the moving of these things would be down to Mother, Earl and myself alone. By the time Earl and Mother had finished moving all father's things down from the loft and into his office it was full to capacity. For the time being I had agreed to keep away.

"Get settled down in your new home and then there will be plenty of time to have questions answered," Earl had said.

Dear old Earl. I was so pleased when I learned he had agreed to continue working as our gardener in our new home. He had always been like a grandfather to me and the thought of losing him as well as my father was too awful to bear. I was even more pleased that not only did he not mind that my father's life was at last to be explained to me, be that he was to be my guide through the journey.

The cottage we moved into had been well decorated before our arrival and after a few weeks, life settled down to some sort of normality, helped considerably by Earl who couldn't do enough for us. That is, until fate dealt us another hand.

The new house had four bedrooms; one was my mothers, another mine and a third was to be used to store most of my father's things. What there was not space for in there was, like at Burrows Cross, put up in the loft. The fourth and final room was left as a spare room and, for the time being, was just being used as a holding area for things not yet allocated a place to live. I was in that room delving through boxes for some books I had temporarily misplaced when I heard Earl clomping up the stairs with his box of tools. Before he appeared at the doorway I heard a curse, followed by a loud series of thuds and a defining crash, immediately followed by a cry of pain. I leapt up and ran to the head of the stairs. Looking down I saw Earl at the bottom of the stairs, the wrong way up, with his tool box upturned and lying on the floor beside him.

"Earl, are you alright?"

"I'll live, young master, but I think I'm a bit bashed up." My mother had rushed to his side and with her help we managed to pick Earl up and, after a gargantuan effort, lie him on the sofa. It was clear however that his leg was in bad shape.

"Damn!" Earl said. "What an old fool I am."

"Nonsense," Mother said, "You've been doing too much." Lie down and I'll call for the doctor.

Chapter 4

Voyage of Discovery

So once again, things had changed. In the days after Earl's accident it was discovered that he had, in fact, broken his leg quite badly and would need to stay horizontal for some time. Earl lived alone, his wife had died in the twenties, and so, with no prospect of being able to look after himself, Mother insisted he stay with us in the, now cleared, forth bedroom.

As once again a routine was established, my mind once again turned to my father. With Earl laid up in bed I took the opportunity to speak to him. "Earl," I said questioningly one Saturday morning, after I had brought him breakfast in bed and sat there watching him eat it for some time. "Would this be a good time to start that conversation?" Earl's face turned serious and he momentarily stopped crunching on his last bit of toast.

"Will..." he started. I could see there was a mental fight going on in his head. Finally, he sighed. "Go and get your mother and then go and do something for a minute." A few minutes later Mother entered and I left and closed the door where I stood and did the best I could to overhear what was said. It was no good, they were speaking in a whisper. After a few minutes Earl's voice changed to normal speech. "Alright, Will, come in if we're that interesting!"

I entered.

Mother was sat at the end of the bed and had a calm yet apprehensive look on her face.

"Sit down," Earl said. I stepped in and sat down on the chair to the right of the bed. "Your mother has consented to me telling you what I know of your father. It will take some time and I will do my best to tell all. When I am done your mother has some things to show you and when you're done with them I have some things of my own you should see."

My heart was racing like a steam train. This was it, the day I had been waiting for for years had finally arrived.

"Now, before you get excited, as I say this will take some time and you will need time to think about what I and your mother will be telling you, and it may be some years before you fully understand it. However, I must repeat what your mother has already told you. Nothing of what we say may be passed on to anybody... nothing."

"I understand."

"Not yet you don't, but you will. There will come a time, William, when your father's story and that of his men will need to be told. But that time will come many years from now, long after I and your mother are gone."

"I will leave you two to talk," Mother said and quietly left, taking the breakfast tray with her and shutting the door as she did so. Earl looked at me and smiled. His big bushy moustache curled up as he beamed at me.

What follows is all I can remember of the conversation, I must have forgotten a great deal though, as our talk went on for many hours but this is what followed:

"So, William. I first met your father in the winter of 1941 at a place called RAF Manston where I was stationed as a warrant officer mechanic with 18 Squadron on the far south east coast. He and a small group of others were sent over to us from another squadron because we were shipping out to North Africa. He was like most young pilots of the time, cocky full of himself and thought he was king of the world; having said that, he did at least have some experience. You see, he had not come from a training squadron, like the rest. He had seen some service by that time in another bomber squadron but not much and I forget the squadron. Anyway, he was a flying officer by then and came over with the sergeants and pilot officers from the operational training units. Your uncle Tom…"

Earl paused for effect and grinned when he saw the incredulous look on my face,

"…was even younger. He was about eighteen and *had* come from training school the pair of them were very close, almost inseparable. Anyway, I rarely saw them and I dare say he didn't even know of my existence for some time after that. So finally, after a few weeks of hanging around finalising the arrangements we moved out and after a great amount of fuss and fuck up's..."

He paused and bit his lip.

"Pardon my French. We ended up in Tunisia. The squadron's job was light bombing in the old Blenheims. They were awful old things; engines leaked, air filters were forever clogging up with dust and the pilots didn't much like them either. Not manoeuvrable enough, and though they were fast compared to anything the squadron had seen in the past, their speed was no match for the kind of aircraft the Germans had in the area.

Anyway, as the months went by, your father proved himself to be quite the leader. He was smart, aggressive and his crew always returned, and nearly always hit something worth hitting. Eventually in mid-1942 your father was promoted to flight lieutenant and given command of B flight. That was when I got to know him better, as I became his crew chief looking after his aircraft 'Q' Queenie. Despite the fact that he was an officer and me an NCO, he talked to me a lot and we became friends, that is, as much as it is possible to become friends in those circumstances.

Then one damn hot day, B flight were sent out on a raid and were intercepted by some Messerschmitt 109's. They were shot up bad. Your father was a little shaken up, well that is, he was very shaken up. You see your uncle Tom didn't fly that mission and the sergeant that flew in place of him was killed, also B flight lost a crew in flames. I could be wrong, but despite the losses the squadron had suffered up to that point, I think that was the day you father realised that the game that they were playing was in fact a serious one and yes, people would die. Anyway, the upshot of all this was that your father needed a few days off and I could see it, so I arranged it so that his aircraft wasn't ready to fly for a few days. We were short of aircraft by that time." Earl winked and grinned. "The CO never suspected a thing. But your father did and although he never said it, I could see he was grateful. By the winter of 1942 things were getting hairy for the crews, losses were up and aircraft were down and there was a certain air of doom in the squadron." Earl looked at the floor. "The next bit of my story I only know because years later, your father told me. "

"He had been called away for a meeting with the top brass at Air Headquarters and had left with the CO, Wing Commander Malcolm. The Yanks had been making their presence known in North Africa by then and they were planning some big operation. They decided, in their eternal wisdom, that they needed a German airfield, near Chouigui I think it was, wiped off the map. So they put pressure on the RAF to sort this out, who in turn put pressure on our CO. Apparently, the CO was keen, as he always was, but your father, seeing the operation for what it really was, was very angry and voiced his protest in no uncertain terms to all at AHQ who would hear him. Unfortunately, his protests fell on deaf ears and the operation was given the go ahead.

So, on the 4th December 1942 your father, and your uncle in their aircraft Queenie and six other crews just like them, led by the CO all took off to attack the German Airbase..." Earl gave a long and deep sigh, he stared out the window now. "And they never came back."

"None of them?" I said, in shock.

"Not one, and that wasn't all. Three more Blenheims from 614 Squadron were also shot down, with all the crews killed. I later found out that your father's aircraft crashed some place near Beja or was it Tebourba far north Tunisia? Anyway, Somehow, he managed, not to just plummet into the ground but got the wings level and pulled up enough to avoid a total wipe out. All three of the crew survived the crash but your uncle and the third crewman, Harding I think he was called, died shortly afterwards of burns."

"Burns?"

"Your father told me that the aircraft burst into flames as soon as it hit the sand. He would also have been killed but somehow he got out, only to realise the other two were trapped. He destroyed half his face trying to get to them."

There was a long pause.

"So, William, why don't you go get an old man a cup of tea?"

As I moved about the kitchen getting the tea ready, memories flashed back. My father's nightmares, what he had shouted, it all began to make sense. 'I told you... I told you. Fire... Get out...' I felt sick. Imagining for that short time the unimaginable pain my father had been going through, mentally and physically. I didn't know the half of it yet!

When I resumed my seat, Earl looked at me as I handed him the tea.

"You alright, Will?"

"Yes, fine, so what happened to father?"

"Well, as I heard it he walked for a day or more and was eventually picked up half dead and three quarters starved by a forward British Patrol. It was bad... very bad."

"What do you mean?" Earl was staring so intently at the floor now I thought he had seen something, and his mouth stayed open as if he was fighting some internal battle again, as if debating whether to go on.

"Your father had dragged the burnt remains of your uncle with him. I heard that when he saw and realised the men around him were British, he shouted and pleaded with them to help Tom, but all they could do was bury him."

I'd gone from feeling sick to using all my muscles to try and stop myself from *being* sick.

"Well as it turned out, shortly before he had left, your father had put me in for promotion to commissioned pilot officer. Coming from him it was taken seriously and with no CO or even so much as a flight commander to disagree I was soon on my way back to England for a spot of leave and some officer training.

I didn't see your father again for over a year. He took a long time to recover from his physical injuries and even longer to recover from his mental ones, in fact, truth be known, he never really recovered from them. The death of Tom affected him badly and I gather your grandparents blamed him for Tom's death. Your father however, blamed to a certain degree the Air Force but most of all, he blamed the Yanks. Years later I tried to tell him it was just war, that these things happened in war and it was nobody's fault, but he wouldn't have it. Wouldn't even hear of it. He was a broken man and you could see it.

Be that as it may, distressed and broken though he may have been, he had not forgotten me. By April of 1944 I had become a senior pilot officer mechanic and was expecting a promotion to Flying Officer any time. I had been working as an aircraft mechanic at a super marine plant in Surrey since my promotion to pilot officer, but I wanted to get back into the action. So, you can imagine my delight when I received a promotion to flying officer and orders to report to number 127 Squadron based at North Wield, under their new CO Squadron Leader, Allen Bennett. The squadron had been bouncing round the world doing its bit and had finally returned to Blighty and been re-equipped with Spitfire IX's in preparation for the invasion of Europe. When I first saw your father again having arrived on station and reported to him, he looked a shadow of his former self. The spark had gone out. Despite that, he greeted me like a long-lost uncle and insisted that I join him for dinner in London, which I did.

Well, the squadron commenced its operations against mainland Europe around May 1944 and the CO was right in the middle of it. I think that was his first squadron flying as a fighter pilot and I remember well how much he loved it. Nothing pleased him more by that time than revenge. One day I remember he was on his way back from a bombing raid and saw a Messerschmitt 109 flying low over the white cliffs. It was headed inland. He later told me that he had fired every round he had into the back of that Messerschmitt, even though the aircraft was completely crippled in half that amount. When the 109 crashed, he returned to North Wield, got his camera and headed out in search of the wreckage. He got back that night looking like a snake that had cornered a mouse.

As I think back now I suppose I should have been worried at the indiscipline or the effect the war had had on the men's minds but I wasn't. There were a few old hands in the squadron like your father by that time. Flight Lieutenant Fitzsimmons was even worse, despite the regulations he would go out alone looking for trouble. Pilot Officer Hector Sharpe should have been locked up if it were peace time. He had had a bad time in Burma and had returned a psychological wreck. Flight Lieutenant McNally and Flight Sergeant Housden were so tired returning from patrol one night they crashed into each other on landing! We were at RAF Lympne by this time. Housden was killed and McNally was nearly killed trying to save Housden. There were many others just as bad or worse and all of them had taken to drinking a great deal more than was good for them and as if all that weren't enough, most of them were gamblers. Between them, they must have lost thousands in the clubs, pubs and bars the world over and this led to problems with the officers' mess bills and all sorts, but anyway all of these men were some of the best pilots I had ever seen and with their kill scores rising and rising the top brass were hardly going to insist that they be taken off active service." Briefly my mind went back to the names I had seen written on the photograph in Father's office, some of them Earl had just mentioned. But my memory switched off as Earl continued.

However, the war was slowly being won and operations decreased to the point that by the opening months of 1945 the whole squadron were expecting the war to end or the squadron to be disbanded or both. I was a flight lieutenant by this time, thanks largely to your father and he was up for wing commander and a desk job. But when he told them he would rather die than take a desk job, they gave him a well-deserved Distinguished Flying Cross instead."

"My father had a DFC?!"

"Yes, I'll show you, but there's so much more to tell you before we get to that." At this point the door opened and Mother came in with another tray, it had been re filled with lunch for two. "Oh, thank you missus," said Earl with a warm smile. "I don't know what I'd do without you."

"I can tell you exactly what you would be doing," Mother replied pointedly. "You'd be up and about fussing in yours or somebody else's garden, fit as a fiddle! But here you are instead!"

"It was my own stupid fault, missus, not anybody else's."

"Well anyway, here's your lunch both of you. Are you learning, William?"

"Yes Mother, and there is a lot to learn."

"Blimey, Will, you don't know the half of it yet," said Earl with a smile.

Mother left again and I sat back down with the tray on my lap so Earl could reach it.

"Well, as I said, the war was finishing and we were all looking forward to going home, at least some of us were. The hardened core of the experienced pilots, including your father, were not looking forward to going home at all. Most had no family, and even less money, and some, like your father, had family but was not exactly close to them, even dead to them, and still more had family but couldn't bear the thought of returning for fear that their loved ones wouldn't recognise the broken wrecks they had become. By this time, we were at B.106 Twente. Holland and the Germans were in full retreat. But then on the 27th April 1945 a large truck arrived and the driver reported to me."

"Sir," he said.

"Sir, I come with orders, where is the commanding officer?"

"Squadron Leader Bennett is in his office," I told him and pointed to the building."

"Thank you, sir," the little officer said and moved quickly for the office. Minutes later the CO came out and walked straight over to me. "Earl," he said in his quiet way.

"Sir I acknowledged him and smiled not knowing what was coming. He looked at me and sighed. This did not look good I thought."

"Earl, how much do you know about Hawker Tempests?"

"Well," said I, "they're big, they're very fast, they're manoeuvrable, though not a match for the Spits, their guns could tear an armour plate to shreds and they drink fuel like it's going out of fashion. Oh, and one more thing, the engine is more complicated than any the whole damn Air Force have in service but what a beauty. I heard it can top two thousand five hundred horsepower!"

"Well we're about to find out if all that's true. We're to be converting to Tempest Fives."

"We could do worse."

"Oh, you haven't heard the best bit yet."

I thought I knew what was coming from the look in his face. We were heading for the Pacific! But I was wrong as it turned out.

"It seems we are no longer needed here. We have been ordered to India, Chittagong to be more precise and from there to operate against the Japs in Burma, though I doubt there'll be much of them left by the time we get there."

"And so we were all on the move again. People weren't overly pleased of course, but they wouldn't have been pleased staying where they were and many would not have been pleased to be sent home, so we were never going to win anyway. One of the pilots, Hector Sharpe, who I mentioned before, was more than a little crazy. Well, he had barely spoken a word since being told we were headed for Burma. I think your father tried to transfer him out but that didn't happen. The one thing in which the whole squadron were united however was its love of our new aircraft. All that is, apart from the mechanics and engineers who had to service them. The Napier Sabre engines were, as I had thought, amazingly powerful but God, were they hard to work on. Although a lot of the problems with the early ones had been ironed out, there was still a way to go.

Anyway, I say we were on the move and that couldn't have been truer; the ground crews, myself included, arrived in Chittagong on the 10th July 1945. The aircraft and pilots arrived on the 12th but it very soon became clear that the Japs had gone, and what few units there still were in Burma had no supply routes or backup. The Empire of the Rising Sun had become the Empire of the Setting Sun by then. We did some reconnaissance patrols and on one patrol we even strafed a small enemy ship, but no sooner had these operations commenced when news came through of the bombs being dropped on Hiroshima and Nagasaki and a few days after that on the 15th August the Japs surrendered. So, after that nobody knew what we were supposed to do. Well, we soon found out, as on the 20th we received orders to proceed to Rangoon in Southern Burma. Well, the aircraft left the next day and the ground crew had two Dakotas put at their disposal and joined the pilots in Rangoon some days later. Some stayed behind to organise the shipping of some of the gear that couldn't be moved by air.

Well, it was about this time that things began to go badly wrong for the squadron. The Monsoon rains had arrived and the weather was appalling. On the 2nd of September, the formal peace treaty was signed by Japan and the war was over. Now you'd have thought that this signalled the end of our troubles and we would all find the nearest bar, but unfortunately it didn't quite work out that way! Some genius at AHQ Bengal, which was itself moving to become AHQ Burma, decided that they wanted the newly peaceful airspace over Japan policed by allied aircraft. The Yanks took it upon themselves to organise this but the RAF, not wanting to be left out, decided it would be a good idea to send a fighter squadron over there to fly the flag. Well, as you probably guessed, that was us.

So, on the 19th of September your father and eleven other aircraft, complete with external fuel tanks took off early that morning, headed for Kia Tak Airbase, Hong Kong. The plan was to land and refuel there, rest a bit, then head to Shanghai, refuel and rest again, then fly the final leg to Iwakuni airbase in Southern Japan, where the rest of us would meet them as soon as it could be arranged. Some would proceed by Dakota again, and some by ship. That was the plan at least!

The twelve aircraft did indeed land at Kia Tak, which by now was also the new home station of both 132 and 209 Squadrons after the formal surrender of the Japanese in Hong Kong on the 16th. Your father's lot *did* refuel and got to Shanghai, they refuelled again and they *did* take off, headed for Japan. But they never got there."

Earl smiled and shook his head.

"Didn't get there? What happened?"

"Well, the details I don't know but your father later told me that shortly after they had struck out over the East China Sea they hit bad weather, very bad. Initially they tried to fly above it and couldn't, then they tried to get under the cloud to maintain some visibility but couldn't do that either so, unable to go around it, they just had to fly straight through the middle, which was very dangerous as they had to maintain tight enough formation to see each other, but not so tight that the turbulence caused them to collide. To add to their problems, because of the haste with which they had been sent off, they had one very bad map and that was it. The orders they were given at Shanghai just gave them a compass bearing to follow in the event visibility was bad. Unfortunately for the pilots and very unusually that day, the storm they were flying through was creating strong winds, blowing from south east to north west but they had been told to expect the winds from north to south, so when finally they spotted a large island, they mistakenly thought they had been blown south of Japan and so altered course and headed north north east for fear they might fly right out in to the Pacific. What they didn't know was that they had missed Japan but to the north not to the south, so by heading north north east they were headed in completely the wrong direction.

Not long after leaving the island behind them they spotted land and, after flying around for a while, were unable to reconcile what they were seeing with their maps. The strong headwinds they had been fighting their way through all the way across the East China Sea had done more than take their toll on the squadron's navigation, it had also taken its toll on their fuel and their gauges finally went into the red. So, with their options exhausted they flew around looking for any town or city they could find, in the hope of finding somewhere to land. You see, the peace treaty with Japan had only been signed a week or days before, depending which country you were in and if they just landed anywhere they could have found themselves under fire from some middle-of-nowhere regiment that hadn't got the news yet.

Well, they needn't have worried about that because they weren't over Japan at all, they were over South Korea which by then was under the Allies' complete control."

At this point my mother entered once more. "I'm sorry to break this up you two but William, I need your help. I need some bits from Peaslake, could you walk over there and get some from the shop?" Now, under any normal circumstance I would have been pleased to run such an errand, but on this occasion, all I wanted to do was stay where I was. Seeing my unwillingness to move Earl piped up.

"Will, we have a lot more to talk about and there's no use even trying to fit it all in to today. We can talk more when you get back."

Seeing that resistance would have been useless I shrugged, got up, and with a "Thanks Earl," I followed Mother downstairs.

As I walked over the hills towards Peaslake, my mind was exploding with thoughts; more than anything, the overwhelming emotion I felt was pride. My father hadn't just been any old pilot who had been bashed about a bit. He was a squadron leader and not only that, he'd fought all round the world from Europe to Africa to Burma and now ended up in Korea. At the time I didn't even know where Korea was, and all this was just what I knew so far. From what Earl had been saying there was much more to come, how much more could there be? The war was over? My mind went back to that day when I had first entered my father's office. I remembered the group photograph with the names written on it. Although I couldn't remember the name, there had been a German name there, where did he fit into all this?

Chapter 5

Pieces of the Puzzle

In light of all I had learnt and as I was in Peaslake anyway, I resisted the temptation to hurry into the shop and then run home straight away and I decided to go and visit Father. I walked past the inn and up the hill, past the church and into the wood. It was a cold spring afternoon with thick overcast clouds that threatened rain and the shadows under the trees gave the place a distinct feeling of late evening but in reality, it was only four o'clock. As I approached the graveyard I walked under the wooden arch that guarded the entrance and stretched out a hand to open the heavy wooden gate. As I did so I looked up into the graveyard and caught sight of a man standing at the foot of a grave near my father's. It was unusual to see people here at this time. Actually wait, that wasn't a grave near my father's, that was my father's. I stopped and stood in the shadows of the arch, watching the man. There was some distance between us but suddenly recognition sparked, it was the foreigner from the back of the church at my father's funeral... or was it? Yes... it was. What on earth was this man doing here and who on earth was he?

As I stood silently watching, the man stepped back, clicked his heels together and saluted my father's grave. There was no way that he could have seen or heard me as I made no sound and was in thick shadow at a bad angle for him to see me, but even as I watched the man turned and looked straight at me. He can't have seen me... could he? I didn't move. The man stood as still as I and his eyes didn't move from my position. Finally, I decided there was nothing for it and stepped out of the shadows, trying to look as if I had just arrived. No sooner had I done that I realised I had little choice but to walk right up to where the man was standing. Maybe I should pretend I'm here to visit a different grave until he goes away? No, if I do that and he recognises me then I'll look even more stupid. 'Oh hell,' I thought and walked toward him. Before I closed the distance between us the man began walking towards me. With about ten yards to go he stopped and stood straight as a rod, facing me. He was a short, very thin man, maybe in his fifties or sixties with jet black hair but his foreign features made it difficult to guess his age, so I might have been wrong. I didn't know whether to say hello or to turn and run. I stopped. The man keeping his eyes fixed on me, had a completely blank expression on his face and, with his arms at his sides so straight they could have been tied to his belt, the man jerked into a bow. Jerking equally fast back to the vertical, the man fixed his eyes over my shoulder now and walking past me as if I were no longer there. He made no sound as he walked and, reaching the arch entrance, he walked through and disappeared from view.

I stood for a moment trying to digest what had just happened. How had he known I was watching? Who was he? Where was he from? China? Japan? Korea? Did they look Asian in Korea? Hang on a minute, had I just seen a ghost? No, of course I hadn't stupid! Pulling myself together I walked the remaining distance to my father's grave and looked at the gravestone. I hadn't been here in far too long, over a month. Despite there being nobody there, I was gripped by that feeling of awkwardness that often comes in these situations, whilst one wonders whether they should say something. Deciding that if Father was watching me from above then he would know what I wanted to say anyway. I decided to say nothing. I stood there in silence studying for the thousandth time every minute detail of the gravestone. The inscription at the bottom of the stone read:

DETRIMENTO·MALIGNITAS·VICTORIA·ULTIO

I had no idea how to say it but Mother had told me what it meant once. I had not understood at the time. I decided to ask on my return. For some time I stood there lost in thought, then a strong gust of wind rushed through the trees and I looked up, closing my eyes as I did so.

My peace was disturbed by a droplet of rain hitting my closed eyelids and I opened them, deciding it was time to go. After getting what Mother had asked for from the little village shop, I ran home, not for the conversation but because I was getting very wet!

When I got in, dripping wet and freezing cold, I shook myself off and took the things into Mother. On seeing me she put on a sympathetic face. "Oh, sorry dear, I thought the rain wouldn't hit before you were back. I should have taken the car."

"It's alright, Mother. It was my fault anyway, I went to see Dad."

"Oh," she said. "I should go up there myself sometime soon."

Deciding not to mention the unknown foreigner I remembered the inscription on Father's grave stone. "Mother, what does that inscription on Dad's grave mean again?"

Rolling her eyes to the heavens, Mother looked at me. "Oh that, well your father asked that that be put on his head stone in his will. I mean, of all the things to put in a will! He called it his motto, it's in Latin and it means, 'In Defeat, Malice, in Victory, Revenge'."

"What does he mean by that?"

"Damned if I know but your father told me once that when I understood that I would understand everything."

"Do you understand it?"

"I think so. When you get the full picture of your father's life sorted out in your head, maybe you will too." I turned to go upstairs but just as I did so Mother said, "Don't go into Earl. He was fast asleep a minute ago when I took him a cup of tea, let the old man rest."

'Damn it,' I thought. But then I had an idea. I went to my room, changed into some dry clothes and went to my bookshelf. I soon found what I was looking for. One of my books gave a very brief overview of all wartime squadrons of the RAF, RAAF, RCAF and RNZAF. I turned and read the quarter page devoted to 18 Squadron. Amazingly, right there was a brief description of the mission in which my father had been shot down. This was not because of the grievous losses the squadron had suffered, very un-patriotic. It was because of the Victoria Cross awarded to the commanding officer. It read: 'Whilst in North Africa, the CO was awarded the squadron's first Victoria Cross of the war for conspicuous gallantry and determination in the face of the enemy. Regrettably, he did not live to receive it.' Well, I thought that's one way of making a total disaster look like a victory!

I then turned to the page on 127 Squadron and here I got another shock. The squadron's glowing history was laid out for the reader, complete with kill scores and a few heroic tales. But confusingly, the final line of the story read: 'In the final months of World War Two, the squadron was disbanded, the pilots being posted to other squadrons, 30th April 1945. (B.106, Twente, Netherlands).' More confusing even than that was that with each squadron, the names of the wartime squadron leaders were written under the squadron story, but my fathers was not there. Could Earl have been mistaken about the squadron number? Very unlikely. Confused and disappointed, I spent the rest of the evening delving through the few Royal Air Force books I had, looking for anything that might help me. Having found nothing and Earl not having woken up, I resigned myself to the realisation that I would learn nothing more until tomorrow. As a last attempt to do something, I opened my world atlas and looked up Korea.

The next morning Earl was awake early, as he always was, so, complete with dressing gown, I went in to see him. Mother was not awake yet. "You're keen," said Earl with a smile and a wink. I explained my lack of success with my books and Earl smiled again.

"Ah, Will, just give me time, all will become clear. So, where was I?"

"Father was over Korea looking for a place to land."

"Oh yes. Well they couldn't find any airfields but they did find some very large fields just east of a large town called Mokpo. And thanks to the strong and stable undercarriage of the Tempests they were all able to land safely. But anyway, I'm going to have to pause at this point and explain what was going on at Iwakuni airbase in Japan. Having heard nothing of the 127 Squadron Tempests that were, by then, supposed to have arrived, and knowing of the storm they had had to go through, the allied brass were becoming concerned. So much so that they sent a message to Hong Kong asking for details. Now it just so happened that I was just arriving there on a Dakota with some of the ground crews for refuelling, prior to carrying out the final leg of our journey. Because the storm was still raging over the East China Sea we were told to set up a bivouac camp on the edge of the airfield and stay put for that night so we could fly to Japan the next day. Most of the crews did just that but I stayed in the command post that night desperately hoping for news, but by the next morning which would have been the 20th we had still not heard anything and in the late morning all twelve aircraft were posted missing, presumed lost in the storm. With the loss of my CO and both the flight commanders I was now the most senior officer left in the whole squadron so I had a meeting with 132 Squadron's CO to discuss what he thought I should do. He basically said that Air Headquarters Burma would have to be told and they could make the decision. So, under his authority I did just that.

While we waited for a response from them I had little to do other than see all various elements of the squadron staff, kit and spares for the aircraft secured and covered on one side of Kai Tak airbase and had it all put under guard to prevent the thieving mechanics from the other squadrons having the lot.

Well, a few days went by, that then became a week and I have to confess I was so miserable all I wanted to do was go home. No sooner had the war ended than I lose the entire squadron to Mother Nature; all my friends and a CO I'd have gone to hell for. The only good friend I had left was a huge Scotsman named Raymond Morgan. He had been a warrant officer and my right hand man for months but then got busted down to airman when he beat the living daylights out of some USAF Captain. He and I sat around drinking tea cursing the RAF for its inefficiency and the USAF just for good measure.

As it turned out however, I was wasting my time keeping our equipment from the other squadrons because after a week of sitting around, orders finally came through from AHQ Burma. I can't remember the wording but the covering page read something like: *'To Flight Lieutenant E. Moore, Temporary CO, 127 Squadron. Sir, in response to your request for orders, I must inform you that due to the loss of all your aircraft and operational officers as of the time you receive this message, 127 Squadron is now disbanded. All remaining ground personnel formally of 127 Squadron are now posted to 132 and 209 squadrons at Kai Tak with a small detachment to return to England as and when arrangements can be made. Lists of aforementioned personnel attached with relevant postings.'* And thus ended my two or so week career as a squadron CO." Earl grinned widely. "Didn't like it much. So all the kit went to the other squadrons and the personnel were split up. Fortunately, only the officer postings had names beside them, the rest were posted by rank or position and AHQ Burma obviously hadn't realised that we were short one warrant officer and up one airman so I took Ray Morgan as my adjutant and quite truthfully told the adjutant of 209 Squadron, to which a crew warrant officer had been posted, that we were short one warrant officer and he would have to find a replacement from somewhere else. I had been re posted to Iwakuni with a flying officer from Air Headquarters Burma, who arrived a few days after the orders to supervise the organisation of the airfield and to receive another RAF fighter squadron at an as yet unspecified date.

So myself, Airman Morgan and Flying Officer Gerard headed for Japan where we arrived on the 12th October 1945 on a Dakota, and would you believe it, we were left there for over five months and surprise, surprise no fighter squadrons turned up! Well, you can imagine what we were all feeling like by this time, and to make matters worse, it was bitterly cold by then. We really had little to do but talk and occasionally make some totally irrelevant and unimportant decision. I got to know Gerard well; his father was English, and his mother was Japanese. The father had worked in Japan as some sort of diplomat but just before the war broke out, sensing trouble, all three of them fled to England. Too young to join the forces for most of the war, Gerard had finally joined in mid forty-four and because of his linguistic skills had been posted to Air Headquarters Bengal which became AHQ Burma from where he had joined me. Fate had dealt his family a cruel hand however, because shortly after Gerard had left England a V2 landed near his parents' house in London, killing both of them.

It made all three of us a bunch of lost sheep really. Ray Morgan had grown up in an orphanage from where he had joined the RAF as soon as he was allowed, and me, well my parents were both gone and although I had some distant family I didn't really know them or where they were.

Anyway, one cold clear morning in early February 1946, with snow coming down in drifts I was sitting having breakfast when I heard the unmistakable sound of a Tempest partially muffled by the snow, and sure enough, as I looked out of the window it touched down on the runway and taxied in. It was unmarked so I assumed it was probably some factory delivery to a communications squadron or something. Actually, speaking of breakfast.." I shot Earl a look.

"Oh, OK but just tell me, was it my father?"

"Good Lord no, it was a heaven-sent angel no less but more on that in minute."

After fetching a simple breakfast and saying good morning to Mother I was back in Earl's room quivering with impatience.

"So, what was the heaven-sent angel all about?"

"Well, initially we didn't know that he was one. He walked in still in flight gear, beating the snow off his shoulders that had already started to settle there. Seeing me and Gerard now in less than pristine officer's uniforms the newcomer asked gruffly."

"Is this the officers' mess?"

"Uh no,", said I. "There is no officers' mess as such. This is the dining hall but you've missed breakfast." Gerard grinned but the grin soon vanished as the newcomer removed his flying jacket to reveal group captain's bars no less! As myself and Gerard leapt up from our table and stood stiffly to attention. The group captain went on, "I'm looking for Flight Lieutenant Earl Moore, he's an engineering officer."

"You found him sir, and this is Flying Officer Gerard." Gerard gave a stiff bow and the group captain's manner changed completely, he seemed to let out a breath relaxing as he did so and a smile crossed his face.

"I have a message for you from a friend," the newcomer said, walking over to me, holding out an envelope. Taking it, myself and Gerard stared at each other in astonishment wondering what 'friend' I could have that was so important that a group captain no less, was acting as his errand boy. Well, I opened it and inside were three letters. The first read:

Dear Earl, I suggest you sit down before continuing, but I'm not dead. Me and the boys are all fine and in good health. I will explain everything when I see you but for now let it suffice to say, I need your help.

If this letter finds you, I ask that you gather whatever tools and Tempest parts you can and be ready to leave on the 20ᵗʰ of February at around eight or nine o'clock from wherever Kilmartin finds you. I will be sending you a DC-3, please tell nobody that we have survived and use the second letter as authorisation for anything you need. I warn you that this is not official and if you want no part in it then rest assured that I do understand. Please destroy these letters and I wish you well. But also know that if you do join us you will be well taken care of and money will not be a problem, I hope this finds you in good health and I look forward to seeing you soon.

Squadron Leader Allan Bennett DFC.

P.S. Please send Kilmartin back with your answer.

Well you could have knocked me over with a feather. As I let out a loud laugh I turned to the second letter:

To whom it may concern, Flight Lieutenant Earl Moore is acting under my direct and personal orders in a matter of the utmost importance and urgency. All officers and men of the RAF are instructed to cooperate in any manner requested by Flt/Lt Moore. Signed Air Marshal A. Bennett CMG, DSO, DFC.

Turning to the third letter I saw that it was an exact copy of the second except my rank had changed from flight lieutenant to squadron leader. 'Fat chance,' thought I and laughed again. Gerard who must have thought from my laughing that it was a posting home looked inquiringly at me. Leaving him in suspense for a minute, I turned to Kilmartin, who by now I suspected was not a group captain at all, and smiled knowingly. 'Tell the *Air Marshal,*' I said with emphasis, 'yes and thank him for his confidence.' I paused deliberately, then added, 'sir.' Kilmartin gave me a knowing look and a deliberately exaggerated smile then turned on his heel and left. So I was right, he was no group captain. So…

"Hang on" I cut in. "Would that letter have worked? I mean wouldn't the Air Force know there was no Air Marshal Bennett?" Earl laughed.

"Bless you Will, by that time the Air Force was so big and spread over so much of the globe nobody knew how many Marshals there were or their names."

So we sat down again and Gerard, looking a little shell-shocked, asked, "What on earth was all that about?" Over the course of the time I had known him I had decided Gerard was a good man. He was loyal to his friends and very clever but he had no particular allegiance to the RAF beyond the fact that that was where he was, and he was making a living from it, and had no real reason even to return to England. Then and there I decided to take him into my confidence. He already knew all about your father from the long hours we had spent talking over all those months of inactivity, he knew also about how hard it had hit me when I thought the whole squadron had been lost. When I explained what I intended to do and asked if he wanted to come he stared at me in disbelief.

'And what would we do, how would we live and don't forget, if we're caught it's desertion. I know the days of firing squads are over but that would not be good!' I assured him that your father would have thought of all that and if he hadn't, well we could extricate ourselves probably before the RAF even noticed we were gone. But I also told him we should take Ray Morgan.

A few weeks later, after a lot of secret conversations between myself, Morgan and Gerard, a lot of trickery of the engineering branch and a lot of packing and boxing up of tools, parts and personal belongings, our little band of three found ourselves around eight in the morning sat once again in the dining hall in winter clothes waiting for the sound of a Dakota that would probably signal the beginning of a new life. We were not alone as the whole room was stacked full of crews, station personnel and civilians of so many nationalities it could have been a UN conference, all of which were having breakfast.

A little after eight thirty the sound of big radial engines boomed around the airfield and as one, all three of us stood up. I had instructed the tower to have the DC3 directed to a hardstand just off the runway where we had secured all the equipment we could beg, borrow, trick and a little we stole out of the various engineering branches dotted around the base, I had even managed to send a Dakota back to Kai Tak for some Tempest parts that I was assured were still there because no more Tempests had as yet arrived in China since your father and his squadron had vanished.

Well, it took the three of us and a handful of ground crew just under an hour to load up all the equipment into the Dakota and, when complete, I thanked the ground crew and hopped aboard with Morgan and Gerard. Ten minutes later we were racing down the icy runway and off into the overcast morning. After about ten minutes of looking at the view I went up to the cockpit and sat down in the co-pilot's seat. I knew the pilot by sight but not by name and he knew me, he had been a new arrival in 127 Squadron shortly before we shipped out of England, but I'd barely seen him before the squadron's disappearance. Shouting above the noise, 'So, what's your name?'

'John Quinn, sir, ex-pilot officer.' The strong Irish accent was unmistakable.

'Earl Moore,' Quinn smiled as if to say 'I know that.' But he extended his gloved hand and we shook. 'Is it worth me asking where we're going?' In response, instead of answering, he simply handed me a map encased in a plastic wallet. To my astonishment I saw a red line across the map. The bottom of the line was marked Iwakuni, from there it headed north north west over the Sea of Japan hugging the east coast of Korea at a distance of about a hundred miles. As the coastline curved more north west, the line followed it maintaining an approximate hundred-mile distance off. The line continued until it stopped just south of the Chinese-Korean Border next to the Changla river and was marked 'Kangaroo?' 'Good Lord,' I thought, 'we're headed for the Soviet part of Korea.'

Chapter 6

North Korean Secrets

If I thought I'd seen snow in Japan then it was nothing compared to the bleak white landscape I saw in North Korea. It was with even more horror, I looked down in the direction Quinn pointed. "Kangaroo airfield!" he shouted over the noise. The airstrip that I could just make out through the blizzard looked to be too short to land a hurricane, never mind a Dakota!

The Dakota's wheels hit hard as Quinn stalled the aircraft into one of the slowest landings I have ever seen but, despite the ice, Quinn held it in a straight line and with almost no airstrip left, the big aircraft stopped. Turning it round to face out towards the strip again Quinn cut the engines and smiled. "Not a big airbase sir, but then the bigger it is the harder it is to hide."

"No aircraft?" I asked for I could see none, nor any bumps in the deep snowdrifts that could have been any.

"All will become clear, sir, shall we disembark?"

As I threw open the side door of the aircraft the first thing that struck me like a sledge hammer was the cold, a bitter cold like I had rarely felt, made worse by the howling wind. The second was the complete silence, only the whistle of the wind over the wing could be faintly heard. The wing was already disappearing under a thin layer of snow and within half an hour the whole aircraft would vanish to the world. I grabbed my personal bag and jumped down onto the slushy tarmac looking around this airfield, if you could call it that! It was in a very strange and well, dangerous location, to be sure. The area of reasonably flat land that made up the airbase was very small for a base and surrounded on three sides by a horseshoe-shaped mountain range. The centre of the horseshoe being the base. The open side of the shoe was the only approach and the option of an overshoot was non-existent as the horseshoe mountains must have topped well over one thousand feet at their lowest and at least two thousand feet at their highest. At this point I was shaken out of my awe as Gerard's considered verdict was delivered.

"Christ, I knew hot hell was down but it looks like cold hell is up! What the hell have you got me in to?" Before I could answer I noticed two figures looming out of the snow. I recognised one of them almost immediately, despite his thick winter clothes. The other was a small, thin man, I assumed to be Korean.

With a smile, your father walked over and we warmly shook hands. It had been six months since I had last seen him but despite his smile he had aged twice that much.

"Earl!" he said and shook me warmly by the hand. "You made it, good man, it's good to see you." He looked at Gerard and Morgan. "Mr Morgan, this is an unexpected pleasure. Decided to join us, did you? Well, you'll be welcome, and who are you?" Your father's face turned stern as he looked at Gerard.

"Flying Officer Jack Gerard, sir. Pleased to meet you."

"And I you. Gentleman, this man has a name I will never be able to pronounce but in this country, they address their personnel by rank, not name, so this is Chungjwa, which is equivalent to a wing commander. He is our liaison officer."

The small man gave a stiff bow.

"Come inside and we'll talk, you must be frozen."

Your father turned and began walking towards a tiny shack at the foot of one of the steep hills that made up the horseshoe. It was covered in snow and the only thing making it visible was the grey door against the white snow. When he opened the first door and then a second I immediately realised that this was no shack. A tunnel led into the hillside and I could already see at least three doors beyond.

"Got a surprise for you," your father said, grinning from ear to ear.

He led us down a long corridor, past a guard room, going further and further into the hillside, through another door and passed two more to the left and right, through another door then took a ninety degree turn to the right and passed five more doors to the left and right, finally coming to a door at the end of the corridor.

"Gentlemen, welcome to Kangaroo Airbase."

He opened the door and we walked through and were greeted by the most astonishing sight. We found ourselves in a huge area, easily the size of a full-size hangar back in the England, though not quite as high. In rows on both sides were twelve Hawker Tempests, each in their own bays, surrounded by tools, spares, and overhead steel girders supporting craning mechanisms and engine lifts. Wandering around were five or six European and Korean mechanics. I remember standing there like a fool with my mouth open. I turned to Gerard and Morgan. Morgan had a thin grin on his face. Gerard, like me, looked awestruck.

"My God, so this was where they ended up," was all I could say. It was immediately obvious that this was not the first time your father had seen this reaction from new crew, and he was obviously delighting in it.

"Yes, indeed. The sea could not have them so the mountains did! Well, let us go through to the mess area and introduce you to some people, then we will talk about your little part in all this, if you wish to stay."

After a last quick look around the hangar we went back through the door we had come through and right into the area your father had described as the mess area. It was a large room about twenty metres long and about ten metres wide. Within the room were numerous chairs and tables at one end with drapes and artwork hanging on the walls. To one side was a bar and the far end of the room from us was laid out like a briefing room. The whole place reminded me of an officer's club back home. Our attention was not on the room but on a small group of men sat around a table close to the bar. Some of them I immediately recognised. Flight Lieutenant John Fitzsimmons and his younger brother Tim were there. Pilot Officer Hector Sharpe, I also recognised; Pilot Officer Quinn, who must have come in another way, and then I saw the 'Group Captain,' Kilmartin whom we had met in Japan, only now the group captain's bars had vanished to be replaced by flight sergeant's chevrons on his arm. All were grinning at us and John Piped up.

"Pappy, how you been, old man?"

They used to call me Pappy when we were back in 127. Your father led us in and up to the little group and introduced us all.

"So some know some but gentlemen, meet my number two and Leader of Red Section Flight Lieutenant John Fitzsimmons or 'V' as we call him, this is Leader of Blue, Flight Lieutenant Joe Price, or 'Reaper', John Quinn 'Irish' you know already, Pilot Officer 'Sniper' Tim Fitzsimmons, and this sorry excuse for an officer is Pilot Officer 'Hectic' Hector Sharpe, Group Captain George Kilmartin or 'Preacher' you know but as you can see he is no Group Captain," he said with a chuckle. "And finally gentlemen, he may be wearing a borrowed coat but this is no Brit. This gentleman, is Oberleutnant Herrmann Metzger and of course, we call him 'Jerry' but don't for God's sake get him talking about aircraft comparisons or you're in for a long day.

"Sorry looking lot I know but they're the best pilots in Korea. And gentlemen," he said, turning to those he had just introduced, "these are Flight Lieutenant Earl Moore, my old crew chief, and one of the finest mechanics in the RAF and his friends Flying Officer Jack Gerard and Warrant Officer Raymond Morgan, another of my old contemptibles." All of us grinning shook hands.

"Good that's done. Now gentlemen," he said again turning to his merry band, "we will leave you in peace as we have things to talk about." He led us over to a table away from the rest and invited us to take a seat. "Can I get any of you a drink? We have most things." After some consideration we all ordered a brandy and started peeling off some of the jackets and jerseys we were wearing, as the room was quite warm. The Korean wing commander had said nothing since we had first met on the tarmac but it was clear that this was due to a limited knowledge of English more than anything else, as he smiled a great deal. Returning from the bar, your father sat down, beckoning us and the Korean officer to do the same and began.

"So, you gentleman are currently sitting in the heart of one of the most secret projects ever undertaken. Kanggye Airbase, known to us as Kangaroo Airbase, as you have seen is almost completely underground with only a small runway that is well concealed. It was built by the Japanese as a line of defence that was never fully finished or used but, as you can see, we have cashed in on their failure. This base has seven full-time European officers, nine if we include you, and with yourself Mr Morgan, seven NCO's, all at the top of their game. We also have forty-four Korean personnel, cooks, cleaners, untrained mechanics, administrative staff etc. As you may be aware, we are in the part of Korea currently under the temporary jurisdiction of the Soviet government. However, I am happy to say that through a combination of bribes and complex secrecy, whilst they are aware of the existence of a small landing strip here, they are completely unaware of the presence of the underground base and us. However, they will not be in charge for ever, and it seems likely that within the not too distant future the country will be divided into two separate countries, North and South Korea. In short, gentlemen, the situation is unstable, uncomfortable and likely in the near future to erupt into either civil war if they're lucky or God forbid, used as a staging point for a war of much greater scale if they're not, and that, gentlemen, is why we are here.

"The temporary government, or council as many are calling it, of North Korea in their wisdom are of the opinion that they are totally unprepared for any kind of war, let alone that which may be coming. In an effort to put together a military force capable of defending the country, the north have brought in advisors from all round the world, especially those with some experience of how wars should be fought and military units should be formed, run and maintained. Some of their efforts are secret and others more public. Now I will say right from the beginning that we are not here as combatants, we are here as advisors in weapons, tactics, squadron structures etc. But for this we use our aircraft. We also will need them if ever it becomes necessary to leave. However, we never fly out with any more than two aircraft at a time and we have only been out twice up until now as the weather has been bad and the aircraft still look like what they are: RAF. We need to change that and as soon as possible as the weather will soon clear and then we are going to have to earn our pay."

Curious about how all this had come about I piped up.

"Sir, if I may, where are the rest of the pilots that left Hong Kong and where did you get the extra few?"

"So your father explained the story I've already told you about the storm and landing in South Korea out of fuel. Well, continuing on from that he explained how they had lined up their aircraft in the field and, leaving most of pilots, your father and Fitzsimmons walked to the town nearby. If I go into all the details I'll bore you but the long and the short of it was that they were approached by a government official there who broached the idea to them and offered to find the fuel they needed to make the journey either north to Kangaroo or south to Japan and back to the RAF. Until the fuel arrived they were wined and dined at the governor's expense. When all preparations had been made the aircraft were flown to Kangaroo, that had only one month before been left by the Japanese, to be shown the facilities and discuss who would stay and if any, who would go. Well, on arrival at Kangaroo and after lengthily conversation seven decided to leave and five to stay, your father amongst them. The seven that left were mostly the ones with families or those who were not done with their RAF careers yet. Apparently, they hatched a plan so that the seven who left were to be taken back to the coast and were to get in touch with the Allies saying that they had crashed into the sea as had been suspected and that they had been picked up by a fishing boat. They had not been heard of since, so it was supposed that the plan had worked."

"He then went on to explain that Flight Lieutenant Price was a Beaufighter pilot with 27 Squadron in Burma but was shot down by an RAF Spitfire, presumably having been misidentified and captured. He had a hell of time in the prison camp and as the Japanese retreated he was loaded onto a ship bound for Japan as work force. However, that was torpedoed by an allied sub and sank, taking his navigator and hundreds of POW's to the bottom just off the coast of Taiwan. Now, for the life of me I can't remember how he ended up in Korea but he too was intercepted by a government official and, with no reason to go home, he was taken north to join us and had arrived only a week or so before I had."

"Flight Sergeant George Kilmartin's story was a mystery to all at the time. He had been at Kangaroo when the squadron arrived and had been a pilot in Greece with 603 Squadron, I think it was, and that just left the ever fiery Oberlieutnant Herrmann Metzger. Now he was one hell of a personality. I later had cause to wonder if that was his real name because I later realised, long after I was back in England, that his name directly translated into English, is Warrior Butcher. Either he was lying about his name or his parents had a warped sense of humour! Anyway, he was the only jet pilot amongst the squadron; he had flown the famous Messerschmitt 262 in Jagdgeshwader 7 towards the end of the war in Europe. But some time before the German surrender he was sent to Japan to act as advisor on the use and tactics of jet aircraft, as it was planned that the Japanese would shortly have large squadrons of jets themselves, mainly thanks to plans and specifications passed on from Germany. Well, although the Japanese did get some jets active before wars end they never made much of an impression and never achieved the vision intended for them, and with the imminent defeat of Japan, Herrmann had a difficult decision to make: wait to be captured by the Americans, risk dying alongside his increasingly hostile Japanese bosses, or flee and hope for the best. Well, he chose fleeing and after stealing an old Mitsubishi Zero he flew north and landed in South Korea. His plan had been to surrender to any British military force he could find but instead, like all the others, the Korean government found him first and he was brought to Kangaroo around the same time as Kilmartin to wait until aircraft became available."

"So gentlemen," your father continued, "now that you know the basics let us now get on to the best and more unfortunate parts of this situation we find ourselves in. First, the bad news. It is just not possible to get you back to England for the time being. If you decide to join us it will be put about that the aircraft that you were flying in to get here is missing, and it will be presumed that you are lost and as such, your RAF life will be broken up and sent to whoever your next of kin are. This makes it possible for you to return when we are done here, whenever that is, under the excuse that you crashed and were lost for however long and, under that pretence, we have an almost limitless amount of time. If you choose not to join us then you can fly back to where you came from and you can announce that the letter requesting you and the equipment was a forgery and you returned, which means you have a few days to play with, and, as I said in my original letter, I will think no less of you if that is what you wish to do.

"As far as our time here is concerned, we are somewhat isolated, it is true. We are free to roam the area and go into the town of Kanggye if we wish and old Chungjwa here can provide each man with papers necessary to explain our existence and get us a little bit of cooperation where needed. We have two vehicles at our disposal which we use to get around and every Friday we all go into to Kanggye for some jollification, although it's been quite difficult lately with the weather. All supplies come to us curtesy of the central council, everything from clothes, to fuel, to potatoes! As squadron leader I am maintaining the RAF military ranking system, uniforms and procedures for the time being but as you've seen we are all friends here, and the ranking system only really applies to operational flying and the little administration we are required to do. As engineering officers I am giving the engineering branch of Kangaroo entirely to you. You will be responsible for the smooth running of the entire maintenance branch and, more importantly, the smooth running of the aircraft themselves.

"As a squadron, we do have a job to do and that means flying on a reasonably regular basis. The aircraft need new markings and the engines will need the same regular servicing that they always did but as you can imagine, spear parts will be hard to come by.

"So, before we get to the all-important question, let me tell you the positive side of this deal. If you choose to stay and act as military advisors in your various fields then the Korean government will pay you the equivalent of one hundred and fifty pounds per month to officers and eighty pounds a month to NCO's for every month you choose to stay and you get paid in either American dollar notes – and God knows where they got them from – or gold, it's up to you."

Again, I found my mouth dropping and my face staring in astonishment at hearing such a huge sum of money. When I looked at Gerrard and Morgan they had an equally stunned look on their faces which quickly turned to a wide smile as they caught my eye. You see, Will, in those days a pilot officer in the RAF could expect around two hundred and fifty pounds a year. So this was a life-changing sum of money, by anybody's standards. At this point, and for the first time, the Korean officer cleared his throat and spoke in a quiet and heavily accented but with good English.

"Gentlemen, my government wishes to show the proper respect for your experience, your knowledge, and your sacrifice in coming here. We thank you much."

Not knowing how to react the three of us immediately whipped the stupid looks of our faces and half nodded, half bowed to the little man. Then came the big question.

"So, gentlemen before I really bore you with the precise details of what we do here, and how we do it, I'm afraid I need an answer. Do you wish to join us?"

Chapter 7

Our New Life

Looking back, especially now, I'm surprised I had made up my mind so easily and quickly. Certainly, I had no appreciation at the time of what I was letting myself in for but that wasn't your father's fault. Nobody there could have known where this was all leading. Anyway, after mere seconds of looking at each other it was obvious what each of us thought and that was that, our new lives began. But I suppose in a way we were the perfect people for the job, no family, no home as such, no life to go back to.

Over the next few days myself and the other two settled down into a routine. The life was good, although we were isolated we were able to relax in a way we had not been able to for years. I now commanded one Korean officer, three Korean NCO's and seven Korean airmen, complimented by five European NCO's and one aircraftsman.

For the foreseeable future my job was to re-paint all the aircraft, destroy all serial numbers and make sure that if the aircraft ever fell into the wrong hands there was no way they could ever be traced back to where they originally came from. We kept one Tempest in the old markings just in case, but all the serial numbers went. As days turned to weeks and winter slowly became spring the snow began to stop and the temperature became more civilised and with this activity at Kangaroo increased. The pilots took out two, sometimes three, aircraft every few days, and flew to bases around that part of the country to train the North Korean Air Force pilots how to fly and fight and with my increasingly skilled bunch of engineers and fitters I kept the aircraft in good working order.

At this point the door opened and mother walked in. "Now you two, you've been at it for hours and I'd say it's time for a break. It's a lovely day and I think you should spend some time outside, Will. Go for a walk or something."

Before I had time to voice a protest, Earl agreed.

"Good idea, missus, I'll send him down in just a moment."

Mother turned with a smile and I heard her walk down the stairs. Turning back to Earl he put on a hurt look.

"Now, Will, don't look at me like I just betrayed you. You must respect your mother's wishes." His face melted into a knowing grin as he continued, "But there is a reason I agreed. I have something to show you which it would now be a good idea for you to see."

Leaning over the side of the bed Earl reached down under it and withdrew a large pouch. Straight away I saw that it was a military-type pouch, kind of like a satchel only without the strap and made of a tough material, like soldiers' webbing. Opening it, Earl withdrew a large thick bound book with the words '*DEVIL'S SQUADRON*' written on the front. Despite Earl's care when handling it, it was obvious that the book and the pouch had seen very rough times. Earl paused, holding the book in a very protective way, rather like a priest would hold a bible, closed with one hand holding the book from underneath and the other flat on top holding it shut. My eyes must have been sparkling as Earl looked at me with a grin. But then very suddenly his face became stern and concentrated.

"William, this is for you. It is the operational record book of the squadron at Kangaroo, but more than that, it is the squadron's and the squadron leader's diary. I have never read it. Your father told me once that he thought he ought to burn it, but he never found the time or the will to actually do it, I guess. Now William, there will be accounts and thoughts in here that your mother would likely be hurt to here, and therefore should not know. It might upset her and I don't want that. She knows about it but has no wish to read it. Lord knows, I probably shouldn't even be giving this to you but somehow it seems the right thing to do. Keep it safe, show nobody!"

"I won't," I promised.

"When you read it, always keep in mind that whatever is in here, your father was doing what he thought right at the time, and like your mother said, he was a good man, never forget that. We still have much to talk about, I suggest that you read the diary for a bit and then we can continue."

"Thank you, Earl."

"Go on get off with you." Replacing the book in the pouch, I picked it up, and with a glance back at Earl I left his room. As I glanced back Earl sat, staring out the window, a calm expression on his face, an old man unburdened of a great load he was no longer able to bear.

Moving quickly to my room I stuffed the lot into my backpack and left the house before Mother could ask any questions and headed for Peaslake. Thoughts pouring through my mind it was all I could do to bite back the temptation to pull out the book, and read on the way. No, I needed peace and quiet. From Peaslake I walked up the long road to the top of Holmbury Hill and there at the top I sat down under the shade of a tree and pulled out the book. My father had been the last person to open this, indeed he had written it!

Operational Record Book

Number 127 Squadron

Devil's Squadron
of the Korean People's Air Force
(Training Command)
(Combat Command)

Commanding Officers:

Squadron Leader A. Bennett , DFC, Order Of The National Flag 3rd Class

Bases:

Kanggye (Kangaroo) Airbase, North Korea
1945 - 1950

Aircraft:

12 X Hawker Tempest V's
1 Douglas DC-3

Aircraft:

Hkr Tempest V D1 (Formally NV941/9N-L)
Hkr Tempest V D2 (Formally NV942/9N-T)
Hkr Tempest V D3 (Formally NV943/9N-S)
Hkr Tempest V D4 (Formally NV944/9N-E)
Hkr Tempest V D5 (Formally NV945/9N-P)
Hkr Tempest V D6 (Formally NV946/9N-R)
Hkr Tempest V D7 (Formally NV947/9N-B)
Hkr Tempest V D8 (Formally NV948/9N-F)
Hkr Tempest V D9 (Formally NV949/9N-X)
Hkr Tempest V D10 (Formally NV950/9N-U)
Hkr Tempest V D11 (Formally NV951/9N-J)
Hkr Tempest V NV952/9N-H
M. Douglas DC-3 44-76382

Compliment:

European:	9 Officers + 7 OR's	(16)
Korean:	4 Officers + 44 OR's	(48)
Total:		(64)

Pilots: 8 - 7 Officers + 1 F/S

Pilots:

S/L Allen Bennett DFC	127 Sqn
F/L Joe Price	27 Sqn
F/L John Fitzsimmons DFC	127 Sqn
O/L (F/O) Herrmann Metzger	(JG7)
P/O John Quinn	127 Sqn
P/O Tim Fitzsimmons	127 Sqn
P/O Hector Sharpe	127 Sqn
F/S George Kilmartin	603 Sqn

Ground Crew:

F/L Earl Moore	127 Sqn
F/O Jack Gerard	AHQ
W/O Raymond Morgan	127 Sqn
CPL Squires	
LAC Lawrence	
LAC Tayleur	
LAC Dean	
AC Adaway	

Looking at the squadron reduced to cold figures in this way made me realise how small the squadron had been, but I was surprised also that, given how much of a secret this whole story was, that this book had survived. Despite all the efforts to disguise the fact that my father's squadron existed, it would have all been for nothing had this book fallen into the wrong hands. The handwriting was definitely that of my father. I turned another page and found a blank page, then turning again the story began.

23rd September 1945

Much like the Flying Tigers Squadron of China in the early days, this squadron is now unofficially officially formed from the few aircraft acquired from the now presumably disbanded 127 Squadron RAF. At the North Korean highly secret airbase of Kanggye as a training unit whose purpose is to train the newly forming Korean People's Air Force of Korea. The purpose of this unofficial Operational Record Book is to record the flights undertaken by the squadron and also to record a squadron diary. I also intend to use this as a personal diary of our time here, in the event this may later prove useful.

Having arrived here on the 22nd we have installed ourselves in our various quarters and have been learning our way around this most unusual of bases. Our hosts are a most interesting people, very generous, very anxious to please, and yet, from the little I have seen from outside this base, it would appear to be a very poor country. The weather here is bitterly cold even now, and there is a thin layer of snow over the whole place. The airstrip is so small that it is difficult to land here, even in fighters like the Tempest and will no doubt take some time to perfect. I have had the pilots up every day to practice but we are told that the winter is coming and the snowfall will be heavy, so I think we will be forced to wait it out until spring. More pressing than this however, is the need for spares, parts, and trained engineers and mechanics to service and maintain the aircraft. Somehow, I need to get Earl, or somebody like him, here to train up all these inexperienced Korean maintenance crews. I am also anxious that the men do not become lazy and so a strict fitness program is to be implemented and when this cannot be done outside, we will use the hangar.

On arrival here we have acquired ourselves two more pilots, including a Luftwaffe jet pilot and five other ranks, all ex-RAF. How they got here I have yet to find out, but even if I asked would I hear the truth? They seem to be genuine in their defection but as I am already learning here, not all is as it seems.

This is indeed a desperate venture; the weight of responsibility weighs heavy on my shoulders as it is me and no other who could have stopped this before it started and chose not to. True, that many were keen to come but some are not. Can we be sure that when they get home they will say nothing of what has passed here? Home. I find myself wondering if I shall ever see it again. Tomorrow we shall decide who stays, and who goes, and the way in which it is to be done. Tomorrow I am also to meet our new Korean liaison officer who will be responsible for the Korean compliment and getting us all we need to sustain us from food to fuel. I also hope to soon develop an idea of how long we are requested to stay here, and how, if at all, we will be able to get home.

24th September 1945

Today a convoy left the base, taking seven of us with them. We are now seven pilots remaining, if you include the two new officers. The convoy brought a Korean staff for the base of some four officers and forty-four other ranks. Commanded by a Chungjwa, *which I think translates to wing commander. He seems a very agreeable man, and is anxious to emphasise, despite the fact that he outranks me, that this is my base entirely to be commanded by European officers. The Korean contingent are merely here to keep the base functioning, cooks, cleaners, guards, though I found myself wondering what they are guarding against? Are they to keep spies out or us in?*

In answer to my previous question of yesterday it seems that we are to stay here as long as we wish. Certainly, if there is a war coming to this land, I do not wish to be dragged into it. I am anxious that we remain as we have been created, a training wing. I am however still uncertain about timescale, what if a war does not come? How long can we realistically live underground? According to our liaison officer, Chungjwa, we are to begin training in a few days if the weather permits. F/L Fitzsimmons and myself will fly to Base One where we are due to meet with senior officers of the Korean army's aviation wing. There are a number of airbases within easy range and the names are of no importance, so I have numbered them instead. Base One, which is to be used as our base for training, is about fifty miles to the south east.

26th September 1945

NV941 S.L. Bennett	**Kangaroo – Base One**	**t/o 09:00**
NV942 F.L. Fitzsimmons	**Kangaroo – Base One**	**t/o 09:04**
NV941 S.L. Bennett	**Return**	**L 16:00**
NV942 F.L. Fitzsimmons	**Return**	**L 16:12**

I met our military and political top brass today at Base One to receive my orders and discuss when, where and how we are to begin our training programme. What few pilots they have are mostly trained in Soviet fighters (saw some Yak's of various types along with some older aircraft) manned by Soviet pilots, though this is not to be widely known. The political leaders, as a long-term plan, wish to separate the army aviation wing from the army to create a Korean Air Force but this will be some time in coming as they are both inexperienced in command of such a force, not to mention very poorly equipped, and even poorly trained so we do have a lot of work to do.

It was widely agreed that until the winter passes, flying will have to be very limited but top brass will be coming to Kangaroo for training in command and control as well as high command structure. For the pilot training we will be flying from Kangaroo to Base One and will be training new and current pilots and crews from there as they are not able to land at Kangaroo and are forbidden to know of its existence anyhow.

One Russian officer who is it seems to be entrusted with the knowledge of who we are, and where we fly from, is a Major by the name of Pamez of the 494th Fighter Regiment. I spent a great deal of time talking to him at Base One, already with kill claims from what he calls the 'Great Patriotic War', it seems that up to the time we arrived he was to try and train the Koreans but he lacks equipment, aircraft and support. However, he makes a great deal of the relationship between the Koreans and Soviet Russia and seems sure that aircraft and pilots will soon be on their way to support him and I assume us. But against who, that's the question?

A DC-3 has been placed at our disposal with RAF markings but I'm unsure that it could land here and until the weather improves I'm not going to try but P/O Quinn would be the logical choice as he has flown DC-3's before.

It is of serious concern to me that I have, thus far, been unable to rectify our lack of competent maintenance staff. We only have two European maintenance staff, CPL Squires and LAC

Lawrence, and neither have experience of Tempest engines, though they are learning fast.

27th September 1945

We are barely into winter yet and already the cold is biting. If Chungjwa is to be believed, were it not for our underground hideaway in a month or so, were we to wander outside our survival would be measured in minutes were we not very well wrapped up.

As I read my father's words, I tried to imagine what Kangaroo Airbase must have looked like. Then, in a moment of clarity, I remembered the photograph on my father's wall back in Burrows Cross. Tempests in rows, under covers, covered in snow. It all made sense, no wonder the size of the mountains confused me. They weren't to be found in Europe after all. I must find those photographs again, and that chest of my fathers, where had that gone? How much prying could I reasonably get away with?

Turning the pages, I saw lists of aircraft taking off, aircraft returning, routine orders, lists of stores, personnel, exercises and all the hum drum routines of a peacetime airbase. Then on the 20th October 1945 I read:

It's no good, today I stand down the squadron from all flying until the spring. The weather here is unbelievable. God, it is cold, you barely notice the sunrise due to the cloud being so thick and it snows and snows. Anything left outside freezes and we just finish clearing the airstrip of snow than we have to start again. Ice build-up on the aircraft in flight is of grave concern and it's hard enough landing on such a short runway without adding surface ice to the equation. I will not lose any of my men, or aircraft, for no better reason than training flights!

21ˢᵗ October 1945

Well, we were brought here to teach, but as we can't do that presently we may as well learn. Chungjwa has arranged for lessons in the Korean language for all the Europeans. Though the idea was greeted with less than passionate enthusiasm, to say the least, I feel it stands to benefit all. So, until spring we will have lessons for one hour every day in the briefing room.

The storerooms are full to busting in preparation for the mid-winter in the anticipation that the stores will struggle to get through. Exercise sessions continue and despite the pale skin of the men, they are looking very fit. I am mindful that if I do not keep them focused they could go mad cooped up in this place for what could well be a long time. I am gratified to say that my continuing efforts to get English newspapers are at last bearing fruit. They are months out of date and often arrive in parts and indeed rarely but they remind the men of home, if indeed any of these men think of it as home anymore? We may make new lives for ourselves in Korea but we cannot stay here for ever.

My father and I had rarely been what could be termed 'intimate' but I could see from his words he was anxious, maybe even worried. I stared out to the South over the hills and thought again of the times me and my father had talked. I realised I never really knew him. I sensed that this story was not going to end well, and even if it did, my father's story I already knew would not. With great determination I resisted the temptation to flick to the back of the book and see how it ended. It was time to head back. I put the book back in its pouch, got up, and started the long walk home.

Chapter 8

The Reason

The crash as the shells struck the wing was huge.

"Shit!" a voice shouted over the radio. "Dodge for Christ's sake, dodge!"

"O Orange going down off to starboard, skip. Christ get us out of here!"

"That Jerry bastard's coming round again, skip... Seven, no, six o'clock now!"

All around me was the *ratatatatat* of guns firing, our guns, and the roar of the engines straining, clawing at the air, desperately giving every ounce of power they could and every few seconds a *whoooop* of bullets whistling past the canopy.

I had no idea what to do, I could see the control yoke in front of me, but my hands were on my knees. I tried to grab hold of the yoke but my hands would only move agonisingly slowly. OK, I have it, turn and pull back hard, I told myself. We were low, so low, 500 feet maybe 400. I looked behind me, as a rattle of machine gun fire peppered my fuselage again, hoping to see the others but I saw nobody, an outline of the fuselage filled with impenetrable smoke.

"Tom, where the hell are you? Report!"

"I'm here, skip. I can't get this Jerry, he's all over the place, and there's two more over at four o'clock. I think were buggered!"

"I'll go for height and we'll bail."

"It's too late for that, skip, you go up he'll have us!"

"He's got us anyway," an angry voice shouted.

"Silence!" I shouted but as I did so another huge crash sounded and the whole plane shook violently.

"Skip, port engine's on fire!"

Somehow I knew what to do now but I just couldn't do it. My hands were not responding or rather they were but so, so slowly. I tried to lean forward to close the distance between my hands and the fire buttons but then another crash and the yoke shook. The sand of the desert quickly filled my forward view, we were going down! Fast! I pulled back on the yoke, straining every muscle I had. The bitch just wouldn't respond.

"Cooome ooon!" I screamed in desperation. "No... yes... no!"

With a sharp intake of breath and sweating profusely, my eyes opened and with a whimper I suddenly realised I'd been dreaming. I sat up, hooked my feet over the side of the bed and sat there trying to calm down. I pulled my father's journal out from under my bed and gripped it tightly. I knew if I switched on my light and started to read there would be no more sleep for me so gently, I put it back under the bed and lay back once more. Then I heard a thud, then another just outside my door. I shot up again as the door slowly opened.

There was Earl, with a crutch under one arm, I could just see his silhouette against a moonlit window behind him. "Now, Will, you alright?"

"Yes, I'm fine," I answered. "I was just dreaming of Father."

"Aye, well, be a fair bit more of that in the coming weeks, I dare say."

"You shouldn't be up, Earl. I wouldn't want you falling down the stairs again on my account."

"Ah young 'un I've fallen down many stairs in my time, metaphorically speaking of course, but I'm still here, aren't I?"

"And thank goodness for that."

"Good night, Will."

The next morning, I brought in a cup of tea to Earl and found him sitting up in bed staring out the window.

"I do love the summer," Earl said.

"So do I, it's the longest holiday I get."

"Aye, well it's going to be a busy one for you till I get out of this damned bed. I want to be out there pruning the roses, not sat here, useless."

"You'll be up soon, and at least you can sit outside very soon, leg up and all."

"Stop jabbering and come and sit down, Will. I know why you really came in." I sat down obediently. "So, how much of that journal have you got through?"

"Well, you haven't arrived yet."

"Oh aye, well I suppose much had happened before me but I knows little of it. But anyway, I should have mentioned before that around the same time as I arrived, although we didn't find out for a long time, something called the North Korean Provisional People's Committee had been formed by this man, Kim Il-Sung. Now, this meant that the country of Korea had been formally split in to North and South Korea and there was no love lost between them, believe me. Now the Russians were heavily involved with the North and…"

"Major Pamez?"

Earl's face showed surprise as he looked at me, then instantly changed to a look of badly concealed hatred. He stared back out the window and through gritted teach growled, "Major Pamez… the devil himself."

There was a long pause during which I could see a wide array of emotions crossing over Earl's face. Finally, he straightened himself and with a smile looked at me and said, "Well, there is much before we get to that. I won't bore you with the political stuff. Suffice to say, we had a routine going the boys and your father flew regularly; week followed week and month followed month. I never got to see the pilots that were being trained but your father told me that they were mostly Korean and trained by our lads and an ever-increasing number of Soviet crews, but our base remained isolated and nothing came or went without your father's say so. Occasionally I did go to the town with some of the men from the base, but not much. It wasn't a nice place. What was though, was the country in summer. Oh lad, you should have seen it. Mountains high as you like, views like nowhere I had ever been, and the river… well, what a place.

As time went by, as senior officer in charge of all ground equipment, I spent more and more time with the Korean liaison officer. He is not like anybody else I met out there, he is a kind man and strange for that time; he was from the far south of the country and had somehow ended up in the north. I assume…"

"Wait, you said 'is'? You still know him?"

Earl looked at me very hard. Then, without shifting his gaze he said quietly…

"Aye… I still know him… and so do you, at least by sight."

Suddenly it struck me. The man at the funeral, the man at my father's grave! How in the world had he got here, and why?

"Aye, that's him," Earl said, grinning at my expression of understanding and shock.

"Known to us at the time only as Chungjwa, his real name is Lee Jung Soon, though it was years before I found that out and even when I did, the Korean names are a strange thing. Very easy to cause offence if you're not careful, so we just stuck to his rank instead, even after we left."

"But?"

"Easy lad, one step at a time. Well, as I was saying, he is a kind man and unlike most around us at the time, not afraid to show it. As time passed his English improved, as did our Korean, and we became friends. He was very fond of your father. Like all his kind, he was a fiercely proud type at the time. He was also a very useful man, if we needed anything it was him that organised it. Every scrap of fuel, food, entertainment we had. The parties he used to organise in the mess, by God they were something, drink, dancing, women…"

Earl suddenly shot me a sheepish look.

"Oh, uh, well, maybe some parts of this story may have to wait a few more years lad."

I grinned.

"It's alright, Earl, I'm old enough to know what happens under those circumstances."

"Aye, well much like during the war the circumstances, as you call them, got monotonous, despite the fun. Years passed."

"Years?!"

"Aye, years. The summers were alright, and productive; we were able to work outside and, under the supervision of myself, Gerard and Chungjwa we had the Koreans extend the runway almost to the edge of the river, making landing and taking off much easier. This also meant that the DC-3 could land, fully loaded, safely, so this sped up the supplies even more. But the winters, Jesus… cooped up underground for months at a time, unable to go out for fear of freezing to death. Anyway, things began to get a little hostile. Our lads began to talk about going home. Even if only for a bit. But I think if they had somehow managed to get home they wouldn't have come back. Chungjwa was sympathetic but it was clear he couldn't let us go. He had his orders and out there you didn't want to go against those. But it was frustrating. See, the Korean ground crews rotated out of the base every year, the guards too, but us, well we were stuck there. Only the pilots flew to other places but even they were watched the whole time.

"Anyway, by the winter of 1949-50 your father struggling to keep everybody in order. Everybody trusted your father and knew him as the good man he was, but they were bored."

Earl looked down and shook his head and let out a great sigh.

"You see, Will, the boys didn't know what to do and even if they had been able to leave. They didn't know where to go."

"Home, surely."

"Ah, well you see there were the papers."

"Papers?"

"Aye, papers. You see, we thought we knew what we were doing and why we were there, but in truth, we had no idea. During the whole time I was at Kangaroo the locals had been sending us newspapers from home, at least, that's what we thought. They were all proper, looked right, and were always dated months before like any genuine paper would have been. What we didn't know was that they weren't papers from home at all. They were fakes made by the politicians in the north to send us false information."

"But…"

"The papers, over years remember, had told us that the United States, having helped win the war, had got so rich and so powerful that they were making aggressive moves all over the globe. The picture they painted was of most countries, including Britain, now in a state of subservience to the US. It told us about how only the Soviet Union, China, North Korea and the remnants of some of the once defeated German, Japanese, and Italian forces still resisted the US and that if they gave in, that the US would rule the world, and with an iron fist. We had been told that although war had not come yet, it might at any time. By way of adding weight to this, the papers had told of policing patrols on land, sea and air by the US to ensure its control. Occasional uprisings, including one in London that had been bloodily repulsed with great loss of life! And anyway, these papers were preaching to the converted, weren't they? Almost nobody on the base had any love for the Yanks. Consider: Your father had lost his younger brother because of a badly thought-out attack on the orders of the Yank top brass. Reaper, Flight Lieutenant Price I mean, he'd been torpedoed by a Yank submarine on his way to Japan only days before the end of the war and saw hundreds of good men drown. Mr Fitzsimmons had had his wife leave him and run straight into the arms of a Yank and naturally this meant that his brother, Lewis, was just as angry. Seargeant Kilmartin, the same for the same reason. Mr Quinn had been bombed by some Yank B26 at Allerona and was lucky to get away but hundreds of his boys didn't. Mr Sharpe was as I said, just mad anyway and 'Jerry' Metzger, well he and his country had just been licked by the Allies."

"So it was the perfect storm!"

"Aye, the perfect storm, and little did we know it but the storm was about to break."

Earl stared once more out the window and watched the slowly rising sun. His face held a sad, almost hurt look.

"What is it, Earl?"

Earl turned back to me, but his expression didn't change.

"I suppose I'm just sad we didn't see what was happening before it was too late." He took a deep breath. "Well, as the winter changed to spring once again the flying resumed of course, and the boys went out in two's as they had before and by this time, my God, they were good. I remember one fine spring day I was walking up a mountain, as I often did, and I looked out when I heard engines and there they were. Your father and Mr Sharpe against, oh, must have been seven or more other aircraft, ducking and weaving in mock combat and damn me if they didn't get the lot. You should have seen them throwing those aircraft around."

"Were they actually shooting?"

"Of course not, no. They just spoke to each other and when one had a clear shot at another, they called out."

"But…"

"Just trust me, it worked."

"Did you ever shoot at actual targets?"

"Well, training-wise, yes. We had dragger targets towed behind other aircraft that we shot at but it wasn't particularly good as a combat training tool. We didn't do any ground strafing, though we did do ground firing to zero the guns every now and again. But every aircraft that left the base did so fully armed."

"Why?"

"It was one of your father's many standing orders, and besides, if we accept now, that at the time we thought what the papers were telling us was true then it was a wise order, as at any time war could be declared and we had to be not only ready but proficient."

"But where did you get the ammunition?"

"Oh, bless you, 20mm ammunition wasn't hard to find and anyway, that wasn't my problem. The Koreans shipped more to us than we could ever use. I remember, I once noticed when I was re-arming one of ours, that the shells were British made, but how the Koreans got hold of it I couldn't tell you. My guess is most likely the Soviets.

"Now Will, perhaps you could go downstairs, make a cup of tea, then take that journal of your father's and go and catch-up with that because we have reached, shall we say, a crisis in my tale, but you should be apprised of the whole story before we go on any further, and so you need your father's take."

"OK." I made Earl a cup of tea, put the satchel over my shoulder and walked out the garden gate headed towards Jesses Lane and Peaslake.

When I got there I climbed up the hill, past the church to the graveyard and was intending to walk straight past and on into the wood, when I caught sight of a figure standing in the area of my father's grave. To my surprise, I realised it was the same man who had been there before, only this time I knew why, and this time I had a name. I remembered Earl's words: 'very easy to cause offence'. I don't know why but before when I saw this man I had sort of assumed that he spoke little or no English. I grinned at my own stupidity. Yes, a person living in this town in the heart of Surrey who doesn't speak English! That's likely! In any case, now I knew that he spoke English well. Was I ready for this encounter, I wondered? Was he, the voices in my head said.
Damn it, what's the worst that can happen? I walked back to the entrance to the cemetery and walked through. I slowed and gently walked towards my father's grave. When I was about half way there, the man turned, as he had done before, and started walking toward the gate and, as before, he would have to walk right past me. I stopped where I had done before, and calmly waited for the man to get close.

"Chungjwa?"

The man stopped only a few paces away, as he had before, with a fixed unblinking face staring right at me. He stood ramrod straight. He had no discernible expression, just the deep lines of age that covered his dark and pockmarked cheeks. Then he took another step forward.

"So… you know who I am," he said very quietly. His voice was strange, accented in a way I had never heard. A deep voice, but very calm.

"I do," I said as confidently as I could.

"I am ... honoured to meet you, Master William. Your father spoke of you but I have never had the pleasure." A cautious and very small curving up of the edges of his mouth. "I am very pleased to meet you." He looked up at the trees and through them at the sky. "I must go, Master William, we shall meet again soon I think." He bowed as he had before and walked slowly past me and out the gate.

Sitting down under one of my favourite trees, I pulled out my father's journal and began flicking through. Putting a stick in at December 30th 1949 so I didn't go too far, I held the thickness in my hands between there and where I had got to before. Earl was right, there was years of entries and information here. I could never hope to read it all and anyway, if there was anything that interesting in this wad, Earl would have mentioned it. Mind you, he did not know what my father was thinking, and this journal did. As I had done so many times before in other books, I resolved to turn each page slowly and methodically, allowing a second or two to scan each page. If I saw anything unusual or that stood out I would give it a closer look. I began turning pages. It was much as Earl had said, and like I had seen before, flights in, flights out, drills, then long periods during the winter months with no flights at all. Hang on, here was something:

18th April 1946

D1	*S.L. Bennett*	*Kangaroo – Base Two*	*t/o 10:05*
D10	*P.O. Fitzsimmons*	*Kangaroo – Base Two*	*t/o 10:07*
D1	*S.L. Bennett*	*Return*	*L 17:08*
D10	*P.O. Fitzsimmons*	*Crashed on Landing*	*L 17:12*

Left late for Base Two today for ground staff training and to introduce another batch of recruits to parts of aircraft. On returning, Tim overshot and had to raise his undercarriage to avoid crashing into the rocks. Earl tells me it can be fixed but at what cost in spares? I have decided the aircraft will be stripped for spare parts as it gives us at least one of everything. These aircraft were never built for airstrips this short. It is early days however and given that this is our first incident after these months, it would seem likely that before too long we will gain sufficient experience to avoid incidents such as this in the future.

Scramble drills all morning. Much work to be done here!

Wait, when was it Earl had arrived? I'm sure it was about this time. I flicked back and forth looking for Earl's name. There it was:

20th February 1946

Earl Moore joined us today, better still, he brought two with him, Raymond Morgan who is most welcome and one other, a FO Gerard, who Earl assured me is to be trusted. It is so good to see him again. Though I must comport myself in the ways expected of a commanding officer and in that way, treat all as one. I can't help but feel an overwhelming relief at having such an old friend here. It makes the burden of command easier. It also means that I can leave all ground affairs to him in the knowledge that it will now be handled as well, if not better than I could achieve.

Having had an informal briefing with Earl and the boys, I have given orders that the aircraft be stripped of their RAF markings and serial numbers and the red star be painted on all. It irks me to be flying under what look like Soviet colours, but as they are the markings of the Korean Air Forces as well, I have little choice.

I sat back and closed my eyes leaning on the tree trunk. I didn't know how this story would end, but I had reasonably sure feeling that it would not end well. Earl's reactions had troubled me. From the looks and sighs, I had realised that this was to be a painful journey. If not for me, then certainly for those involved. I read through many pages but learned little I didn't already know. It was interesting to see how the papers that Earl had mentioned sometimes cropped up in the reports my father wrote.

14th March 1947

More scramble drills today, not actually getting up of course but massing at the holding area. We are nothing like fast enough yet.
The papers inform us there has been an incident in the English Channel, between one of our ships and some aircraft of the USMC. Many were killed. 'Our ships'. I suppose what I mean is British ships. I do miss England, but by the sound of it there may soon be no England to return to. Damn it, I will never live under a US flag!

Under this entry a large NEVER had been scrawled with a pencil stabbed into the paper so hard it had gone through to the next page.

10th June 1949

| D1 | S.L. Bennett | Kangaroo – Base One | t/o 08:47 |
| D1 | S.L. Bennett | Return | L 16:30 |

Had a long day of briefings today covering the intelligence relating to types of aircraft now operated by the USAF and USMC. It seems that P51's, F4's, B26's, B50's are still very much part of their fighting force, but with a large quantity of unknown jet types, both bomber and fighter, either available now or shortly. They also have these new-fangled Heliplanes or some such. Aircraft that take off vertically and don't have wings but a huge propeller. We have no idea of their fighting capability.

Maybe instead of staying here until any training is over and threat of war has ceased we are instead to stay here until our aircraft become so obsolete that they, and we, are of no further value. I intend Jerry to give a lecture on the pros and cons of jet aircraft verses prop tomorrow. Not that he has not done this before but I want every weakness of these new aircraft fresh in the minds of all the pilots.

There was so much here, it felt to me like it would take as long to read and digest as it took to write. The more I read though the more I had the impression that my father felt he was losing control of the situation he found himself in. Like he was being pushed towards something he couldn't see, and therefore didn't know what to be afraid of or, if indeed he should be afraid. Earl had said the squadron had not been content by the winter of 1949 and that was underlined by what I was reading;\ fighting amongst the ground crew, even the officers, gambling on a grand scale, drunkenness, the list went on. It was a bizarre circumstance; nine officers and seven NCO's, all rich as lords by this time, entertained, fed, and homed for nothing and yet cooped up in an underground prison that they were unable to escape and didn't even know if they should bother for fear that what was back home waiting for them might be worse still. Even as I thought that I heard distant thunder.

It was time to head for home, and swiftly. I walked briskly down the hill and through the village but as I passed the Hurtwood Inn, the door opened and a man was thrust through it, falling as he did so and landing hard on the forecourt with the door slamming behind him.

"God damn your eyes, can't a man get more than a few drinks in this middle of nowhere hole!" the man shouted in disgust. He had clearly had more than a few already, and not even eleven o'clock. The man remained sat and looked around him. Sighting me he shouted, "You, young sir, is there somewhere a man can get a drink in this place?"

I walked over to him and grinned.

"It's some way to the next pub, sir."

"God rot their bones! What about accommodation?"

"Not much of that either, sir." The heavens chose this time to open and the rain poured down. The man looked around.

"For the love of Christ, call this a bloody summer!"

"I can offer you a cup of tea and some shelter at least for a bit, my home is ten minutes' walk away."

"That's uncommonly decent of you, young sir. Oh well, tea it is then, lead the way. What's your name?"

"William... or Will to my friends."

"Well William, I'm Hector." The man's speech was slurred, and his movements unstable as I helped him up and we set off. After a short while we reached the end of Lee Hollow and started down the tunnel of trees towards my home.

"Where are you from?" I asked, hoping I wasn't being indelicate.

"From? Well I'm from a lot of places, young sir, but I came down this morning looking for an old friend. Apparently, he lives around here some place but after I walked here from Guildford I suddenly realised I didn't know where to start so I tried the pub, and one drink lead to another and so on, you know how it is."

"You walked here from Guildford? That's a long haul."

"Yes, it bloody was too."

"So, who did you come here to find?" At this point we rounded the final corner and there was my house.

Even as we did so, the door opened and my mother shouted, "Come on, Will, get out of this…" She paused as she realised I was not alone. I opened the gate and we jogged the last few yards to the front door. For all the good it did us, as by this time we were thoroughly soaked. Saving introductions till the door shut behind us I turned to Mother and explained the situation.

"Oh you muppet," she scolded. "Look at you, go and change this instant. I'll see to the tea, come in to the kitchen, sir."

As I walked through the kitchen I was surprised to see Earl sat at the table. He turned to face me just as my mother and Hector walked in. I saw him stare for a moment, he froze and gaped with a look of sheer astonishment on his broad face. I looked at Hector and his face wore the same expression.

"Good God all bloody mighty," Earl said in a very faint whisper, and then louder, "What in the name of all that's holy are *you* doing here?"

Chapter 9

Combat

"I, ah, well…" Very confused, but seeing Hector evidently flustered and embarrassment, I tried to help.

"I found him outside the pub in a spot of bother, and offered him a cup of tea and some shelter for a bit."

"Aye, you would have done. Getting into a spot of bother at the pub is something this trollop knows a great deal about!" Earl seemed genuinely angry but there was a touch of fear in his voice, or was it uncertainty?

"His name's…"

"I know his name, Will, now go and change your clothes like your mother asked."

I fled. When I came down a few minutes later, I found mother pouring the tea and Earl and Hector sitting at opposite ends of the kitchen table, staring at each other intently. Clearing his features Hector looked at me and smiled.

"Ah, the young master returns."

"Sit ye down, Will," said Earl sternly. I sat down and looked from one to the other, utterly bewildered.

"What's wrong, Earl?" my mother said, a worried expression prominent.

"I'm sorry, missus." Earl let out a long sigh and straightened himself. "By way of a formal introduction missus and Master William Bennett, this is Hector Sharpe, former officer and pilot of my squadron and now I dare say a penniless, alcoholic, ne'er-do-well, last I heard, of Yorkshire." I stared incredulously at both of them in turn, my mother's face now showed downright dismay and fear. Hector giggled like a schoolboy.

"What are you doing here, Hector?"

Controlling his giggles and smiling a warm smile, Hector leaned back in his chair.

"Well, to put no finer point on it, um… looking for you."

"Why?"

"My dear fellow, there is no need to be so hostile. I mean no harm, bring no bad news. I heard of the tragic passing of one of the finest gentlemen it has ever been my pleasure to know, and wished to come and pay my respects and in addition, knowing you were close, hoped I could find you at the same time and see how you were. Nothing more."

Looking at my mother and me in turn, Hector's face assumed a look of sorrow.

"My sincere and deepest condolences to you both. Allan was a good man, I will miss him."

"As will we all," Earl said with a lighter edge to his voice.

"Thank you," Mother said.

"So, what are you planning on doing?" Earl asked, his brow clearing a little.

"Well, in your frightfully sympathetic description of me you weren't far wrong; short on money most of the time, alcoholic, most certainly. So, all I need is a place to stay, preferably where I can find a drink and maybe we could spend some time talking of the old days, raise a glass to absent friends, that sort of thing."

"The only place like that round here is the one you got yourself thrown out of, or Shere, which is a bit further."
"Dear me, it appears I may have to do some apologising to the landlord then. I return to Yorkshire on Tuesday but I'll have to walk back to Guildford. So, two nights or so, plenty of drinking time."
Earl sighed again.

"You needn't walk back to Guildford, you can get a train from Gomshall which is much closer but anyway, like most things, Hector it might have escaped your notice, but I am presently a bit busted up and can't go walking about the hills."

"We have overcome much bleaker problems in times gone by, Earl, really."

Later that night saw Hector in the Hurtwood Inn, Mother asleep and me talking to Earl in the kitchen. "So, you're up to date?"
"More or less."
"You didn't read any further?"
"No." There was a long pause. "What happened, Earl? Why is everybody afraid?"

"I will try to explain. You see, although we didn't know it, whilst we had been carrying on training, the very country we stood in had been divided and we were in the north and therefore the Soviet side. Worse still, a war had begun, and we didn't know a thing about it. All we were told was that if we saw unidentified aircraft we should be aware of the possibility they may not be friendly, so to use caution. When we pushed for information we were only told that the Americans had got so powerful that Korea itself was now at risk. But your father's orders were clear: we were there to train, not to fight, and if strange aircraft were sighted we were to hide and not engage either from ground or air. Anyway, in June of 1950, everything changed."

"What changed?"

Earl shrugged and almost as an afterthought said, "Why, the war arrived. Look Will, I'm sorry but I feel real tired. Tomorrow I have asked Hector to come here for breakfast, and your mother is going out. We will talk about what happened in depth but Hector is in a better position to explain what really happened. He was in the air with your father, I wasn't."

"Sure, Earl."

Next morning Mother drove to Guildford for some things she wanted and Earl, me, and Hector sat round the kitchen table. Hector, clearly pre-warned by Earl, had arrived with a much more sullen attitude than he had before. He had sat down quietly at the table and both he and Earl had accepted the cups of tea I made them. Then a silence had fallen, broken suddenly by Hector.

"So, I understand you know our secret?"

"I do."

"But not all of it clearly, otherwise I would not be explaining."

"No, after my father died, Earl and Mother agreed to tell me the whole story and we are working through it."

"And before you ask," Earl cut in. "I decided since you had showed up to wait to explain what happened in June of 1950."

"Ah." There was a brief pause "Very well, so on the morning in question, three of us were going over to Base One for a large combat training exercise. Your father, myself and Sniper."

"Pilot Officer Lewis Fitzsimmons," Earl put in for my benefit.

"Indeed. The idea was that your father and a Russian CO would fly high above and judge the outcome and myself and sniper would take on four of the not so useless Korean pilots we had been training for some time. I think it was by way of an exam for them. They were not too bad. We were weaving between mountains for a while, went up a few times, threw the aeroplanes about a bit and in the end all four were deemed as having been either shot down or sufficiently damaged as to be unable to continue the combat. Anyway, that completed we landed at Base One and refuelled and then took off and headed home. We were flying low, your father leading of course, sniper on his right and behind and myself on snipers right and behind, Echelon formation we called it. Maybe ten minutes out of Base One your father saw them split seconds too late....

12th June 1950

"Jesus, brake."

A rattle of machine gun fire splits the tranquil scene. The third aircraft in line receives hits on the starboard wing as the whoop of bullets flies around them. The line of bullets then runs right down the centre of the second aircraft as the first pulls hard up and to port.

"Shit, brake, brake, sniper go low, hectic split S, now."

"I am skip, but the sniper's gone."

"What!" Throwing a glance back, the lead pilot sees only wreckage of what had been his number two floating down, most of it on fire. With rage lining every word, he says, "Where is he? What is he?"

"Skip four aircraft, no six, high at my two o'clock, two more low coming around on you. There P51's, what the..."

"Then get them off, by God I will make them sorry, by God I will!"

"Skip, go low round the mountain to your three o'clock, go all the way round I'll go the other way and take them head on."

"Kangaroo, Kangaroo this is Delta 1, receiving?"

"Delta 1, Kangaroo."

"Kangaroo, Delta 1, sound scramble, repeat, sound scramble, get them up, RVP, line to Base One we are engaged, Delta 7 is down."

"Delta 1, roger, sounding scramble."

"Hectic, coming around any second."

"Pull up hard, I see you, I see them."

Not machine guns but cannon fire now burst out of the leading edge of Delta 6's wings. Taken completely by surprise, the two Mustangs had no time to react, and the leading aircraft took fire and smoke billowed from its exhausts. The port wing root took multiple hits and the wings folded up like a butterfly. As Delta 6 shoots past the second aircraft, Hector pulled hard up and over in a huge loop, then half rolled and came down fast to give chase to the second Mustang.

"Skip, where are the rest? I don't see them."

"I'm leading them towards Kangaroo, they must have lost sight of you"

"I'll finish off this little pipsqueak then I'll be right behind you."

"Stay low." Muttering something under his breath Delta 6 pulls level turning hard left and falls in behind the second Mustang. "Oh, bless him, he's lost me." The Mustang began a slow climb to the right, just as cannon shells run from wingtip to wingtip, many striking the cockpit.

Kangaroo Airbase looked like a disturbed ant's nest. A loud siren sounded as pilots and ground crew poured out of the quarters into the hangar area. As the first engines began to turn over, the hangar doors slowly opened streaming bright light throughout.

"Delta 2 to all aircraft, line up outside, report when ready. Delta 2 to all aircraft, line up outside, report when ready."

Aircraft began rolling out of the hangar under their own power, something never done, unless absolutely necessary. With its pilot Flight Lieutenant Price still repeating his orders to report, Delta 2 spun to port and lined up at the strips top as reports began to come in.

"Delta 3 ready."

"Delta 4 ready."

"Delta 5 ready."

And then finally, "Delta 8 ready."

"This is Delta 2, I have the lead, follow me up climb high and fast to the south east. Delta 2 to Kangaroo, information please."

"Delta 2 Kangaroo, inbound aircraft 6 P51's. Delta 1 and Delta 6 in running fight, down line to Base One"

"Jesus, looks like it's real thing time, gentlemen, you know what to do." One by one the Hawker Tempests tore into the air. "Up, up, up gents, I want to be above these bastards when we sight them. Delta 2 to Delta 1 do you read, skip?"

"Delta 2 this is Delta 1, bandits on my six o'clock. I'm staying just ahead, will be with you in about five minutes. Bandits at three thousand feet."

"Roger, Delta 1, we'll be ready."

"Delta 2, this is Delta 6 I have them at my twelve o'clock. I am in pursuit at distance, sun is dead ahead."

"Delta 3 to Delta 6, Hectic, where is Delta 7?"

"Delta 6 to Delta 3, I'm sorry, he's down."

In a screaming outburst, "God damn it!" Then even louder, "GOD DAMN IT! I'll bloody murder them!"

"Delta 2 to flight, silence if you please. Climb, I want to be at ten thousand for a dive on the bandits from the sun, then wing over and come back at what's left. Form line abreast real tight, pick your individual targets. Be careful of Delta 1 ahead and Delta 6 behind. Search for them, gents, find the bastards. I'm sorry V, truly."

"Delta 3 to flight, none of these bastards gets away, none of them!"

"Tallyho, Tallyho, I have bandits twelve o'clock, low inbound."

"Well spotted, Irish. Right, gentleman, nice and easy, here we go. Stay in formation till we're past them."

Crackling over the radio came the German accent of Jerry. "Just like the old days."

"Wait for it, wait for it." With propellers screaming the Tempests bore down on the unsuspecting Mustangs right out of the sun. Finite adjustments were made to their approach and a grim smile of pleasure tugged at the lips of many.

"FIRE."

Five fingers pulled triggers as twenty cannons spat hate at the American formation. Cannon shell riddled the formation and the Mustangs quivered under the onslaught. The lead aircraft burst into flames, two more had their wings torn clean off them, and thick black smoke spouted from the exhausts of another one with its propellers shattering instantly. The Tempests tore through, pulling hard up. As the G-force crushed the pilots into their seats the flight as one, winged over and now over a thousand feet above and behind the bewildered and terrified remaining Mustangs, prepared to dive down again. Forming into a pair and diving for the mountains, the Mustangs tried to get away but now with Deltas 1 and 6 joining the fight the whole Devil's Squadron dived down after them.

"My bird, my bird!" Fitzsimmons shouted and fired a long burst at the desperately turning Mustangs. His shots hit the engine cowling of the second and smoke billowed behind the crippled aircraft. Metzger, having gained a fraction of a lead on the rest of the flight, also fired and the lead Mustang stopped turning and began a slow roll, steepening his dive until finally the squadron pulled up as the Mustang buried itself in a mountainside.

"Delta 1 to squadron, form up on me in line astern and return to base. Delta 1 to Kangaroo?"

"Delta 1, Kangaroo."

"Kangaroo, Delta 1 bandits destroyed, we are returning. I want all aircraft in the hangar and total defensive camouflage up as soon as it can be done."

"Delta 1, roger, already begun." One by one with remarkable speed and precision the aircraft landed and taxied straight into the hangar whilst the waiting aircraft circled overhead. Finally, the hangar doors crashed shut and camouflage nettings were strung over the space.

I leaned back in my seat, dumfounded. Earl and Hector were studying my face. I couldn't believe it. "So… you destroyed an entire US Air Force squadron?"

"No lad, just a flight, but yes, they all died," Hector said. "In the days that followed the action the Korean army found every one of the aircraft and all the bodies were taken to Base Two; one major, one captain and six lieutenants."

Earl cut in, "I had never seen your father so angry. As soon as he was out of his cockpit he walked to the centre of the hangar shouting for all officers and non-commissioned officers to go to the briefing room. When we got there he wasn't there so we waited talking a bit and poured Flight Lieutenant Fitzsimmons a very stiff drink, kind words that sort of thing and then your father finally came in."

"He looked like a ghost."

"That he did."

"Gentlemen, I have just got off the phone with Base One. I spoke to Mayor Pamez and I want to brief you on current events."

A deathly silence fell on the room as the ten officers and a dozen or so NCO's stared at Squadron Leader Bennett.

"It seems, gentlemen, that a war has begun between Korea, China and the Soviet Union, against the United States only hours ago. Word reached Base One just as I was taking off. The United States has attacked in the south by sea and has already gained a great deal of ground. Their aircraft, both bombers and fighters, are carrying out offensive action all over the country and it was one of those squadrons we met earlier. I am to pass on hearty congratulations and thanks from the Soviet detachment and also from the Korean government.

"Now, as you will all be aware, our role here was supposed to be a purely training one. Today however we have lost one of our own and in response to that, we undertook to engage the enemy and made them sorry. However, we have now been formally asked by the authorities here to undertake henceforth an offensive role in the war to come." A murmur spread around the room.

"Fine with me!" growled John Fitzsimmons.

"I have not given a response as yet but Major Pamez is on his way here by road with ammunition and ordinance, together with more troops that will double the guard on this base, and I wish to have an answer for him before he arrives. Gentlemen, please be under no illusions, as of today we are in harm's way. I want nobody outside unless ordered to be so by me. I want this base invisible from the air. That is all for now, gentlemen. I want to see all pilots, Mr Moore and Mr Chungjwa in the operations room now, please."

The meeting broke up and the men that had been ordered moved into the operations room. When they were all in, the door was closed and locked and Squadron Leader Bennett stepped into the horseshoe of men that had formed.

"Grab chairs, gentlemen, please and sit yourselves down."

When everybody had sat down Bennett sat himself down and spoke in low tones.

"So, gentlemen, you know the situation. I need to hear what you wish to do. Unlike in times past, you are not under orders, and I want a discussion on how we proceed."

"Killing Americans," Metzger chuckled.

"What's to discuss? I'm in," Price spoke up.

"What is the British position on this, sir?"

"We don't know, nor do the Russians but given the news in recent months it seems likely that they will be forced to join the Americans," Kilmartin spoke up.

"It seems to me, if you'll forgive me, sir, that if we are going to fight then we should do so under a similar agreement to old times, we will fight but on the understanding we do not fight against our own people."

"Indeed, George."

"Do you really think that the Korean authorities are going to give us a choice?" Flt Lt Moore asked.

"Chungjwa?" Bennett said turning to him. Chungjwa was finding something on the floor very interesting but he spoke quietly.

"I do not believe my government would be pleased if you did not."

"In other words, gentlemen, our options are fight… or flight? None must stay behind, either we all go or we all stay, which is it to be? I would say that this is not, as I see it, an open and shut option, we do have the opportunity to work something out later if the circumstances change."

"Circumstances be damned, I'm staying." Growled Fitzsimmons through gritted teeth.

"Is there anybody here who wishes us to leave? Frankly, now?"

Nobody spoke.

"Very well, I will speak to Major Pamez and we gentlemen," he said with a long sigh, "shall go to war. Please go and check all your aircraft, report any damage to Mr Gerard or Mr

Moore, I want those aircraft ready to go at a moment's notice. Get to it, gentlemen."

As people rose and began to file out he said, "Mr Moore, Mr Price would you stay for a moment please."

As Moore and Price resumed their seats, Bennett looked at them through strained eyes. "OK, gents, we stay but I want you two to work on a plan that you must, be clear, keep to yourselves. Put together a bulletproof plan to get us out of here should the need or the inclination overtake us."

"Where do you want to go, sir?" Price asked.

"Gentlemen, I have hidden nothing from you. You know as much as I do. Japan maybe? Burma? India?"

"Sir, our aircraft will barely fly that far, Japan maybe, but not Burma or India and what of the ground crew?"

"I know that, damnit!" Bennett growled in a sudden show of anxiety and frustration. "We can get the DC3 back here if we can camouflage it. But put a plan together, tell nobody, not even our boys, and report to me when you have something."

"Yes, sir, should we not include Mr Fitzsimmons?"

"Yes, but don't trouble him with it now, he needs some time."

"Sir."

"To your duties, gentlemen, thank you."

"Your father knew something was wrong, I don't know how he knew but he did. Not only that, but he knew who to trust and who not. I never did understand why but he knew Chungjwa was to be trusted." Earl grinned. "It was Chungjwa who arranged for Tim's body to be brought to the base where we buried him with full honours. The Koreans provided a huge honour guard. Chungjwa who also, less than a week later, arranged for the DC3 to be flown back to Kangaroo where a special area had been made for it, almost invisible from the air. Not only that, but my lads and I stripped out the inside and fitted more fuel tanks internally. By the time we were done it was a flying fuel tank. Better still, Chungjwa talked the Koreans into believing it was for flying fuel to Kangaroo should it not be possible by road... I suppose that's why your father trusted him?"

This last was said with a deeply considering look on Earl's face.

"In any event, everything changed after that. The base got a lot more cramped as soldiers had arrived en masse to guard the base and fortify it. But your father was adamant, nothing to be visible from the air, people included. Some training was still done at Bases One and Two but this became much more of a laborious procedure as now your father insisted on a minimum of six aircraft at a time in case we found more enemy formations."

Hector cut in. "My kite was busted anyway, so I was grounded as your father didn't want to use the spares unless he really had to. It took Earl days to fix my wing. Mind you, that gave me time to paint on my new kill markings. By that time, I had German, Japanese and American." Hector chuckled like a child. "That always did annoy Jerry."

"Well, it was a month before we clapped eyes on the enemy again. The war, which had started well for the Americans, began to go wrong for them. They were pushed back with heavy losses. Although your father had agreed to fight for the Koreans and alongside the Soviets, he had made it clear we were to be used in a defensive role, not offensive and being as far north as we were we felt reasonably sure that we wouldn't be seeing much of the enemy. But in August we were sat down to breakfast when the CO bursts in."

14th July

"All pilots to the briefing room. Ground crew, get the doors open, and the engines started. Move, gentlemen."

Men tumbled out of the room and the pilots went through the side door into the briefing room.

"Sit down, gentlemen, as quick as you can. Right, we have a job. American aircraft are, as we speak, making an attack on Base One. The Soviet detachment are in the air, as are some of our Korean lot. Many have been lost and we are ordered to assist. So, the enemy are made up of B26 Invaders escorted by F4 Corsairs. These are formidable aircraft, gentlemen. We have the slight edge on speed and firepower but only just, so watch your backs. I will be leading Mr Price's section with Mr Quinn as my number two, Mr Price will be with Mr Metzger, as numbers three and four. Mr Fitzsimmons will be with Mr Sharpe and Flight Sergeant Kilmartin. Stay low, gentlemen. If you get into trouble weave the mountains, its where we have the advantage. Questions? No, let's go."

Pilots filed out into the hangar where their aircraft engines were already running. As the engineers jumped out and the pilots jumped in, Delta 1 was already rolling through the doors. Within minutes the squadron was airborne and at full throttle the aircraft raced for Base One.

"Delta 1 to Delta 3."

"Delta 3?"

"Delta 3, take your section south east, circle round the base and come in from the south."

"Delta 3, roger." Ahead a black column of smoke bitrayed the fight ensuing only minutes away.

"Delta 1 to Red Section, stay low, stay together, and engage on sight, report bandits when in sight." Flying only feet off the ground, the two flights converged on the base. "Delta 1 to Red Section, Tallyho, Tallyho, bandits at one o'clock high, twin engine, looks like the bombers. Blue Section engage the escort, Red Section concentrate on the bombers. Good luck, gentlemen." As Red Section crossed the threshold of the base they broke into pairs and climbed, curving hard to port and formatting on a flight of four American B26's. Instantly the cannons of the Tempests exploded into life and at a range of less than a hundred feet they couldn't miss. Shells exploded right down the length of one of the bombers, but with little immediate visible result as Price and Metzger rolled in behind the bombers and more shell strikes rattled down on other bombers which had been taken completely by surprise and now turned in all directions in an attempt to escape.

"Delta 3 to Delta 1, I see Corsairs to the east, turning in to engage."

"Delta 3, roger." Bennett's head looked for a split second behind him where he could see a melee to the east of the field indicating that Soviet or Korean aircraft were still in the fight. As Red Section broke away from the bombers scanning the skies for threats, a terrific explosion boomed up from the airfield as one of the bombers ploughed into the field. Red Section turned and split to make another run on the three remaining bombers, one of which Bennett noted had its starboard engine afire.

"Delta 1 to Delta 3, how are you doing?"

"Delta 3 to Delta 1, engaged with eight Bandits with four friendlies. Enemy are good, sir!"

"Delta 1, roger, Delta 1 to Delta 2, break off and go to aid Blue Section with the escort."

"Delta 2, roger."

"Delta 1 to Delta 5, stay with me and forget the aircraft on fire, go for the bomber to our one o'clock, I'll take the one at twelve."

"Delta 5, roger." Altering course slightly Quinn lined up meticulously on his target. He fired almost at the same time as Delta 1 and the result was instant. As shells tore into the starboard engine of the luckless bomber it caught fire, and as it did so the wing folded up and detached from the engine, sending the bomber spinning. Bennett meanwhile had hammered his fire into the tail of his bomber and as he did the aircraft suddenly pulled hard up. Continuing until it was vertical the aircraft stalled and as the nose dropped, figures were seen throwing themselves free of the stricken aircraft. Spitting defiance, a top turret rattled off rounds in return fire and Bennett felt his aircraft shake.

"Shit." Even as he said it, Delta 5 cut into his thoughts.

"Delta 5 to Delta 1 you're streaming fluid."

"Delta 1 to all aircraft, report bandits."

Reports came in, but from them there seemed to only be a few fighters remaining and they were running.

"Delta 1 to Delta 2, take command of the squadron. I'm damaged and must return. Keep your eyes open, there must be more of them somewhere."

"Delta 2 to Delta 1, roger. Good luck, Delta 5, escort Delta 1 home."

"So what happened to the others?"

"Well, one by one they all returned to our base. Your father and Mr Quinn first of course, then Mr Fitzsimons…."

"With me and Preacher and then about half an hour after that Reaper and Gerry."

"Indeed, Mr Metzger had been well shot about. He was lucky to make it back at all. Your father was furious cos he and Mr Price had landed at Base One but had been stiffly told by Major Pamez to leave and so had to take off again, riddled with shot and return to Kangaroo. Strong words were had between bases you may believe. Mr Kilmartin was also damaged but not badly."

"What of the Americans?" Sharpe piped up again, with a grin from ear to ear.

"Well, none of the four bombers your father had seen got away, they all crashed either on or near Base One. As for the fighters, I shared two Corsairs, one with Preacher and another with a Korean Yak 9…"

"Mr Price and Mr Fitzsimmons got one each, didn't they?" Earl asked.

"Yes, they did, and Fitzsimmons got another damaged. The rest either ran or were shot down by the other friendlies, I don't know. We later found out that your father was right, there had been many more but some had been shot down by the Soviet and Korean pilots and some had left before we arrived. What we saw was merely the tail end of the attack. We certainly made a mess of them."

"Aye, and they made quite a mess of you, too." Earl harrumphed with a disapproving stare. "Kilmartin had been damaged though not badly, in all fairness. It took me almost a week to get the damage patched up, and it cost me more of my spare parts… for all the damn good it did!"

I looked at Earl who had a hurt look on his face. "Why do you say that?"

Hector cut in with a giggle. "Because then we went and buggered them up again."

Earl, with a venomous look at Hector continued.

"Suddenly the war had stepped up a gear, you see. It didn't last for long, but it was hot whilst it lasted. Only the next day we were scrambled on an intercept when a flight of fighters was in the area. I'd had the crews working through the night fixing damage but Mr Metzger and Mr Kilmartin's kites were still busted so they took Delta 9 and Delta 11 instead."

"And that day was quite an education."

15th July

"Delta 1 to all aircraft, report when ready."

"Delta 2 ready."

"Delta 3 ready."

"Delta 9 ready."

"Delta 5 ready."

"Delta 6 ready."

"Delta 11 ready."

"Delta 1 to all aircraft, get up and climb fast, heading south east, echelon if you please. Delta 1 to Kangaroo, talk to me." Gerard's voice came in.

"Delta 1, Kangaroo, enemy bandits spotted by ground forces approximately five miles south east heading west, moving fast, altitude approximately thirteen thousand. Information comes from Base One, three and a half minutes ago."

"Delta 1, roger. Keep your eyes peeled, gentlemen, these could be jets. Climb to fifteen thousand, and we'll see if we can dive on them."

Engines roared, drowning the scramble horn as, one by one, Tempests swung onto the strip and tore down the hill and up into the cloud laden sky. Minutes later, the squadron was flying through thick cloud in a steep climb slowly executing a wide turn to starboard to fall into line with the expected position of their prey. The cloud was very patchy, with large areas clear then back into cloud. The aircraft cautiously slowed their climb and scanned the skies as they passed fifteen thousand…. nothing. It was near impossible, one minute in thick cloud, the next in a wide pocket of clear air. Then suddenly Metzger's voice pummelled the ears.

"Tallyho, Tallyho, bandits at two o'clock low, six I think, heading the same as us."

"Delta 1, roger. I see them, fighters."

"Delta 5 here, their jet's alright."

"Delta 1 to all aircraft, Delta's 2, 5 and 11 remain at this position, observe and only attack if the need arises, or if I call. Do not lose sight of us. Delta's 3, 9 and 6, follow me in line abreast. Let's go, we'll need everything we've got to catch these boys."

Throttles in emergency power the aircraft pushed into a steep dive. It was hard going, but the Tempests had the speed, and were slowly gaining. The airframes shook as the aircraft approached their maximum speed and the noise of wind rush was enormous. Finally, they reached the same height as their prey but would soon start to fall back for lack of power.

"Delta 1… FIRE!"

Surprised by the order, the Tempests opened fire at longer than ideal range but the effect was instant. Tightly formed as the jets were, it was difficult to miss. An aircraft just off the centre instantly exploded, another swerved hard to starboard either out of control or through sheer panic and collided, with a sickening crash, straight into another. As the wreckage was thrown all over the sky, more random strikes showed on other aircraft but seemed to have no effect as the three remaining aircraft scattered in all directions.

"Fools!" Metzger's voice came over the radio, incredulous. "All they had to do was power up and dive." One aircraft, having turned as hard as it could to starboard and pulled up, had slowed as a result. Metzger, on the inside of the curve, followed with Sharp alongside him. Easily leading his target, and with a perfect plan view of it, his cannons roared out and as shells hit the starboard wing it tore off and the hapless aircraft span out of control. Meanwhile, the two other jets were climbing fast and Bennett and Fitzsimmons had no hope of catching them. The leader was executing a slow climbing turn to port, ensuring that he kept up enough speed to distance himself from his pursuers and eventually would put him in a good position to dive on these impudent prop aircraft. What he did not know was that he was turning right into field of fire of the much higher, and thus far unseen, Price and his flight.

"Delta 2 to Delta 1, request permission to engage Bandit at your two o'clock high."

"Delta 1 to Delta 2, roger, then return to fifteen thousand."

"Delta 2, roger."

Price's flight immediately dived and turned a fraction to port lining up on the jet as it turned under them. Just at the critical moment, the flight flipped their aircraft on their backs and pulled back on their sticks. The aircraft plunged earthward, rapidly gaining speed. As they pulled up they were right behind and just above their quarry. Quinn and Price fired together and shells struck all over the jet. Flames emanated from several places at once, and the aircraft became more engulfed until finally, with a roar, it fell to pieces, creating a huge fireball which as it quickly dissipated left only pieces, both small and large, falling to earth.

"Delta 1 to all aircraft, does anybody see the last bandit?"

"Delta 3 to Delta 1, last saw him run in to that cloud bank to the south, south, west climbing fast."

"Delta 1 to Delta 2, please return to height as quick as you can and sing out if you see the bugger."

"Delta 2, roger, nearly there."

Gradually, the squadron re-formed, and slowly turned, setting a course back to Kangaroo, but saw nothing of the last fighter.

"Delta 1 to all aircraft, we must climb above this cloud and look around, we can't take the chance that that jet will follow us home."

Steadily the flight climbed higher and higher. Passing seventeen thousand feet, they finally reached thinner cloud and the visibility increased, then they were clear. Heads turned in every direction but there was nothing to be seen.

"No leader, and fight blown to bits, he's long gone," Quinn's voice crackled.

"Or he's pissed and looking for revenge," Sharpe replied.

"Bandits! Three o'clock!" All heads turned.

"They aren't jets, skip."

"Silence!" Bennett shouted.

Now at eighteen thousand feet, they were above the unidentified squadron and it was big. At least twenty aircraft, as far as Bennett could see, all fighters. Even as he looked the entire mass of aircraft turned toward them and began to close.

"Line abreast, gentlemen."

Only seconds from an all-out clash that would almost certainly end with the death of every pilot in his squadron, Bennett's eyes began to pick out details. Suddenly, he knew.

"Delta 1, break off their friendlies!"

Turning away from the approaching aircraft, they allowed their identity to be seen and the threatening squadron turned and formatted on them. Bennett made out the aircraft of Major Pamez and dipped his wing in salute.

"Delta 1 to all aircraft, let's head home. Give them a show. We will split S"

As one, seven aircraft rolled over and, maintaining perfect formation, pulled up, diving away and heading home. Half hour later the last of them were rolling up the runway and onto the hardstand.

Earl sighed again. "It couldn't last, of course"

"What do you mean?"

"Look, William, put yourself in the American's place. If you discover an area where there are a bunch of above average enemy pilots. What do you do?"

I looked at him not understanding.

"You send in some of your best and stamp them out. So that's what they did. As the weeks passed they flew over our base in large formations, time and time again, and they didn't even know it."

"Don't forget the medals," Hector piped up.

Earl shot him a withering look, and with a deep sigh. "Yes, yes, the damn medals."

"Medals?" I asked, puzzled.

"Sometime between that last fight and the next, I can't exactly remember when, word reached us that the base was to prepare for a visitor of some importance. Oh, the place was in turmoil I can tell you but nobody knew why or for who. Then, this aircraft touched down that I hadn't seen before and two Soviet and three Korean officers climbed out. I didn't know who they were, except one was Major Pamez but from the amount of decoration, they were clearly very senior. Anyway, Chungjwa stepped over and bowed and the officers ordered us to turn out the station. So we do, and with them all lined up and at attention the officers stood out in front and began to smile and laugh, then they gave some longwinded speech about how we had done a good job, and they wished to recognise some of their *heroes*." Earl invested this word with cold contempt.

"Chungjwa was translating for them, but he needn't have bothered as most of us understood enough by then to hold a good conversation but anyway, they called forward your father and pinned a medal on him. Then, as he stepped back they called Mr Metzger, then pinned one on him. There was lots of saluting and honours but that's about it really." Earl said this last with a reproachful look at Hector.

"They presented us with some flag as well, only small but I believe it represented some sort of honour to the squadron as a whole," Hector said with a grin.

"Anyway, as I was saying, the skies had been busy but we were hidden away waiting for the call, when the enemy made an attack on Base Two, probably hoping to draw us out again…"

"And it worked." Hector cut in again. "We were asked for help again, and again, we went. As before, we separated into two sections as soon as we took off. Kilmartin was ill so he stayed behind, that left your father, Quinn, Metzger and Fitzsimmons in one flight, and myself and Price on our own. Our job was to fly low to Base Two with the rest up high. We had been doing some tactical training with the Soviet and Korean pilots you see, and as a unit it was decided that our squadron was best suited to take on the escort fighters of any attacking force, and Soviet and Korean fighters, the bombers. The plan that day was that me and Price would link up with a hodgepodge of a Soviet flight and two Korean and then signal your father to launch the attack all together. As soon as everybody went into the attack, me and Price would link back up with our lads and fight it out."

"Did it work?"

"Not exactly!" Earl said bitterly.

"What happened?"

Hector sighed deeply and looked at me with an intensity I found unnerving. Then he stood up, undid the buttons of his shirt and slid the shirt off his left shoulder revealing a terrible scar which had long healed but left a significant portion of his arm and shoulder missing. "Not exactly doesn't quite cut it. It was a bloody disaster for us."

Chapter 10

Losses

20th August

"Delta 1 to Delta 2, any sign of those friendlies yet?"

"Delta 2, negative, should be any minute."

"Delta 1 to Delta 2 we have you in sight, we are at your seven o'clock."

"Delta 2, roger."

Seconds later, Delta 1 caught a flash of light out of the corner of his eye to the south west. Snatching his head over, his blood ran cold. Just below him and about a mile away he saw four dots moving very fast, headed straight for Price and Sharpe. The speed of the dots was staggering, these were not propeller aircraft.

"Delta 1 to Delta 2 bandits coming down on your six o'clock, fast!"

Even as he said it he knew it was too late.

The German accent rang out, "Delta 2 brake hard to port! Brake!" Metzger shouted.

Delta 2 and 6 tried to brake but it was too late as four jet fighters bore down on them. The rattle of cannon fire split the peace and Delta 2 shuddered as the shells struck home, Delta 6 also took fire and a shell tore a gaping hole in the side of the cockpit blasting shrapnel all over it, significant portions striking the pilot. With an ear-splitting roar the four jets shot past so close that the turbulence shook the aircraft around violently. Delta 2 was in very serious trouble. Most of his controls had been shot away and smoke, glycol and fuel streamed out behind the aircraft. Too low to bail out he had no choice but to try and crash land. Delta 6 was not in a much better position. Bleeding badly, he half rolled and dived for the trees getting as low as he could.

"Delta 6 to Delta 2, you there?"

Silence...

"Reaper, damn it, answer me!"

There was no response.

"What did you do?" Hector bit back angrily.

"What could I do, for God's sake. I ran for home, of course. But I had to make sure I wasn't followed or it would all be up for us, so I weaved in and out the mountains with the kite behaving like a double decker bus and my engine heat rising and rising. Until finally I realised I couldn't make it so I crashed in a field about a mile from the base. Amazingly, the kite didn't blow up."

"And the others?"

"Delta 1 to Red Section, engage those bastards!"

Red Section pushed their noses down and opened up their throttles to emergency power. The jets had broken into two pairs and spotting Red Section climbed to intercept.

"Delta 1 to Red Section, brake."

Red Section also broke into two pairs of two. They may have been slower but they were above their opponents.

Metzger's voice broke in.

"Remember, turn tight, gentlemen, and they cannot follow, turn tight!"

"Delta 1 to Red Section, do not go head to head. DO NOT go head to head. we don't know the spitting power of this type."

Despite his words, the two formations were indeed coming around for a head-on approach but, on hearing the order, Red Section half rolled and dived away. One jet latched onto Metzger's tail but as he tried to line up a shot, Metzger grinned, closed his throttle completely then rolled to starboard, pulling hard back. As the jet shot past him, he rammed the throttle full forward again and continuing the roll now flipped back, allowing him a few seconds behind the jet. His cannon roared out. In one cataclysmic explosion the jet disintegrated falling in pieces from the sky.

"Got you, you Yank bastard," Metzger growled.

"Wow, nice shot Delta 4," Fitzsimmons shouted, exultantly.

"Delta 1 to Delta 3, bandits at your five o'clock split S…"

"Anyway, within the hour we had damaged another two and with them the third fled the fight. Quinn was hit, but not badly and Fitzsimmons too. They went low and hedgehopped their way back to Kangaroo. We found out later that one of the jets crashed near the north west coast."

"What happened to Base Two and the plan?" Earl groaned.

"The bombers with fighter escort reached the base, and, having done damage, the Ruskies finally attacked after seeing nothing of us. They got a few and lost a few but the base was not badly damaged. It was only a small attack. But we didn't know that at the time. I was just leaving the hangar to go and get some food when Gerard ran up saying that we had damaged aircraft coming back and two lost. Well, we got the doors open and waited. Some minutes later Mr Quinn and Mr Fitzsimmons touched down and by the time they were in the hangar, your father and Mr Metzger were on approach. On their way back, they had spotted Hector and a party of soldiers, engineers and a doctor had been dispatched to do what they could."

"Took them a bloody age to find me and I was only four miles away." Hector said with obvious discust.

"Anyway, no sooner had the hangar doors closed and your father was barking. All pilots."

"Pilots to the briefing room, please."

Exhausted men tumbled out of their aircraft and, dropping their gear, wandered discontentedly out of the hangar and in to the briefing room, closing the door behind them.

"Have a seat, gentlemen. Mr Quinn, be so good as to get Mr Moore and Mr Kilmartin to come and join us."

Seconds later the door flew open and Kilmartin, looking pale and horrified, walked in, staring at the assembled men, searching. Earl Moore was just behind him. Kilmartin looked as if he was close to tears.

"Reaper? Hectic?"

"Have a seat, gentlemen."

Heartbroken, Kilmartin collapsed into a chair.

"So, we have no definite information at the moment but as far as we could make out Mr Sharpe is alive but hurt, and we should hear back from the rescue party soon."

Kilmartin showed visible relief.

"I'm very sorry to say however that Mr Price is lost to us." Quinn elaborated. "I saw him hit the ground, hard, and he blew up, from what I could see he almost pulled out but he was too low."

"He was a good man, and will be sorely missed. But we carry on."

"Do we?" Quinn asked cautiously.

"Are you saying you no longer wish to, Mr Quinn?"

"No skip, what I am saying is that since this fight began we have lost two pilots, possibly three, and three aircraft. At this rate of attrition how much longer can we reasonably hope to continue? I'm not afraid, sir, it's just…"

Bennett cut in. "I know you're not John, and you *do* make a good point. I would have you all know that the flying I have seen you all perform in recent engagements is some of the finest I have ever seen. I know you will have reservations about where this is all leading." He sighed deeply but maintained his fixed gaze at Quinn. Then he looked at the others one by one. "I will think on it… Mr Moore?"

"Well, sir, if we accept that Mr Sharpe's kite is at least heavily damaged and is better used as spares then that leaves us with five serviceable aircraft. Mr Fitzsimmons and Mr Quinn's aircraft are in need of repair with NV591 still in its old colours. All told, in a few days, eight aircraft and increasingly few stores and spare parts."

"Very well. Now to other matters. None of us know what those aircraft were today, but we do know the following, they are jet powered and fast, they sport possibly four cannon in the nose, their climb rate is impressive, but as we suspected, they cannot turn with us. I will find out if Major Pamez knows any more. Gentlemen, I fear that we will be unable to get above this menace and we have learned today that flying low gives them too much of an advantage. We will have a gathering regarding tactics in two hours in the mess. In the meantime, report your damage to Mr Moore, go get cleaned up, get a stiff drink in you and we will meet in the social area later when I will hopefully have more information for you and with luck we will have news of Mr Sharpe. Thank you, gentlemen."

The men rose and headed for the door.

"Mr Moore, Mr Fitzsimmons, a moment." Together they walked through to the operations room. "How's that plan progressing, gentlemen?"

"Well, skip," piped up Fitzsimmons. "The Tempests are out, everything in their range is held either by the Chinese who would arrest us, or the US who would view anything in range of Korea with extreme suspicion, and anyway, the ground crew would be stuck here."

"Can't say I'm thrilled with that option," Moore said with a smile.

"That leaves the DC3, with the extra fuel. We could all get well away but even then mostly American occupied options. Should be far enough away that we could probably bluff our way through though, but through to where? Australia? Burma? Who's to say the Americans don't control them as well? If the papers are to be believed…"

"Yes, that's just it."

"Skip?"

"Are they to be believed?" He sighed. "We need information from outside. Yanks, British whoever? Somebody that doesn't have a vested interest in keeping us here?"

Fitzsimmons looked at him with a puzzled expression. "You think the papers are lying?"

"I have no idea, damn it. I have no reason to think they are but… well… I don't know." He had a touch of anger in his voice and frustration on his face.

"Your father knew it well before the rest of us, maybe suspected it? I don't know but he knew something wasn't right. Either way, we were in a pickle, and we knew it. Anyway, hours later Hector here was brought back and he was in a bad way. As many parts of his aircraft that could be were brought back over the next few days. But by then everything had changed again."

At this point the door opened to reveal Mother with her arms full of bags.

"Afternoon, you lot. Give me a hand, Will."

I helped bring the bags in and put away the food. Then Mother suggested we move into the lounge, so she could make some lunch and to Hector's utter delight, she had brought beer back with her.

"You're a grand lady, to be sure you are," he giggled taking two and planting a big kiss on her cheek to Mother's evident shock. "Hector." Earl said gruffly. "Thanking you missus we shall move."

Sitting down in the lounge I pressed Earl. "What had changed?"

"Well your father had had a long conversation with Major Pamez and had news of the war. The Americans were on the run, pushed right back to a small area in the bottom of Korea. The way your father put it, it was like the war would soon be over. But in private conversations with me it was clear that he wasn't sure that the Russians were to be trusted. But what the Russians had said that *was* clearly true was that action in the far north where we were would likely decrease to nothing, and that it did. We saw no enemy aircraft for over a month, which seemed to confirm Pamez's story. Joe Price's body was brought back to the base and berried alongside Tim. That was hard."

"Indeed, it was, very," agreed Hector. "By the end of September, I was pretty much back to flying as normal and training at Base One and Two had cautiously resumed, though we always went as a full unit, just in case. We had decided on always flying in pairs, spaced well apart, and at staggered heights but we never saw anything. The boys had been up several times at the request of the Soviets to intercept bombers and fighters but I was not with them and anyway, they either never found the enemy or the enemy were too high and too fast to reasonably catch. Until early October."

Earls face showed a cold smile. "Yes, that was when we finally got what we needed."

1st October

The winter was closing in, and at Kangaroo base the nights were closing in, and although there was no snow yet, the cold was bitter. It was mid-afternoon and already almost dark. Overhead, five aircraft circled as one touched down hard and rolled off the strip into the holding area. Just as a second was coming in on its final approach, the relative calm was shattered.

"Delta 8 to all aircraft, Bandit, single aircraft to the south approximately 4,000!"

The aircraft coming down, suddenly powered up to full throttle as its wheels began to come back up.

"Delta 1 to all aircraft, close on the aircraft and identify. Delta 5 stay on the ground, get into the hangar and close the doors."

"Delta 5, understood."

Staying low the five closed with the unidentified aircraft. Metzger's voice crackled over the radio.

"Delta 4 to Delta 1, he hasn't seen us, no avoiding action."

"Delta 1 to all aircraft, stay low."

"Delta 4 to Delta 1, I think it's a Lightning."

"Delta 9 here, If that's a Lightning, I'm a Dutchman, no chance. Definitely American though, I can see the markings, twin-engined."

"Delta 3, roger, so do I."

Slowly the formation closed in as Bennett tried to catch them up. Then the enemy made a slow turn to port, curving back round the way he had come. They followed.

"Delta 3 here, My bird."

"Delta 3, Delta 1, hold your fire. Delta 1 to Kangaroo, receiving?"

"Delta 1, Kangaroo."

"Kangaroo, Delta 1, fire the airstrip flare."

"Delta 1, Kangaroo, confirm, fire the airstrip flare."

"Do it!"

"Delta 1, Kangaroo, roger."

Only seconds later a bright red dot shot up in the gloom just off to the bandit's port side and only about a mile distant. Immediately it turned toward.

"Delta 1 to Delta 3, hold your fire until he's close to base and DON'T miss." This last was spoken with a burning intensity. Seconds later… "fire when ready."

"Delta 3, roger."

Fitzsimmons was at pistol shot below and behind the bandit. Pulling up a fraction, Delta 3's cannon roared out. At that distance the enemy had no hope of escape. Shells peppered the aircraft from end to end and even as they did so the aircraft rolled over onto its back and began to descend. Seconds later, parts were seen to fall away and within a few more seconds parachutes blossomed, floating slowly down not five hundred yards from Kangaroo.

"Delta 1 to Kangaroo, bandit destroyed, send out the guards to pick them up immediately. Be sure to tell the guard I want them alive!"

"Delta 1 Kangaroo, roger, understood."

"Delta 1 to all aircraft, land as quick as you can."

One by one the aircraft landed and as the hangar doors closed the CO and Moore walked out into the holding area as a troop of Korean soldiers aggressively pushed two slumped figures out of the darkness, one clearly staggering.

"Talk in Korean only, Earl, do you hear?"

"Sir."

As the small group approached Bennett peremptorily ordered the guards to take the men to the briefing room.

"Go in ahead," Bennett whispered to Earl. "None of our lads are to show themselves. Tell Mr Metzger to meet me in the operations room, quick as you can."

"Sir," Earl said, and vanished. Minutes later saw the two prisoners under guard in the briefing room and Bennett, Moore, Gerard and Metzger in the operations room.

"Now listen well, Mr Metzger" Bennett whispered. "We are going to go in there in a minute, only you will talk in English, understood?"

"English?" Metzger asked, then seeing Bennett's expression quickly added, "Yes, sir."

"The rest of us will be acting as interrogators and I have no intention of being gentle." Piercing the others with a malevolent stair he added with venom, "You show nothing, understood? I don't want these two knowing who we are, or anything else for that matter. I want information and I will get it if I have to carve them up to do so."

"Sir," they said as one.

"Very well, follow me."

The door opened and the four men walked in. In the centre of the room sat the two men tied to chairs, an armed guard stood by both. One man, in his forties, Earl suspected, was bleeding badly from his shoulder and gazed round with a look of angry resignation. The other, in his mid-twenties, was darting glances from left to right, clearly terrified. Earl and Gerard sat down at a table whilst Bennett pulled up a chair to face the two. Metzger stood beside him.

"Get out," Bennett growled at the guards in fast Korean. One began to protest but Bennett shot to his feet spitting words at them with a look that would have made a viper sheepish. The guards left and Earl rose, relieving one of a pistol as they walked out and locked all the doors one by one. As Bennett resumed his seat he spoke in angry Korean. Metzger translated, speaking to the two pitiful figures in heavily accented English.

"Who are you?" the younger of the two stuttered.

"Carter, 1st Lieutenant, United States Air Force."

"You?" Bennett fixed the older man with a stare.

"MacKinnon, Captain," the man said through gritted teeth.

"I'm going to ask you some questions. If you don't answer them or you lie to me, I won't do anything as nice as kill you. I will do far... far worse. Do we understand each other?"

The younger looked at the older who spat at Bennett's feet. "Fuck you!" he said with pure hatred on his face.

The younger said nothing and stared at the floor. Bennett let out an exaggerated sigh then turned to Earl and Gerard and in Korean said, "Take him into the operations room then through the kitchens and lock him in the guard room. See that the doctor looks at that shoulder, then come back as you have gone. When in the operations room scream like hell, wait a minute then fire the gun and scream again, and again, then come back in."

Gerard roughly dragged MacKinnon out and, whilst the little piece of drama was played out, Bennett sat silently glaring at Carter who looked as if he was about to faint. When the shot rang out Carter jumped and starred pleadingly at Bennett, shaking from head to foot. After the screaming had stopped and Moore and Gerard had re-entered and resumed their seats Bennett calmly spoke through Metzger.

"What were you doing here?"

Carter blurted out, "Armed reconnaissance, sir."

"What aircraft were you flying?"

"North American F82 twin Mustang, sir"

"Where have you come from?"

"Sir, I…"

"Where have you come from?" Bennett spat.

"Sir, I…"

"Point that gun at his knee," Bennett growled at Earl.

With a badly disguised horror on his face, Earl rose, cocked the gun and held it against Carter's knee.

"No, please, Suwon, sir, near Seoul… please"

At that moment there was a loud knock at the door. Bennett nodded and Moore went over and opened it. It was the senior officer of the guard looking like he had just woken up and clearly angry. He spoke in quick, angry tones. Bennett spat words back and gestured him to get out but he didn't move, instead barking more angry words. Just then a hand came out of nowhere and slapped the officer across the face. Turning to see who had hit him, the anger melted away and was replaced by fear as Chungjwa stepped into sight. He growled at the guard who hastily bowed and fled. Chungjwa entered the room and Moore closed, and locked the door behind him then resumed his seat.

"Korean only please, Chungjwa," Bennett said swiftly.

"What's going on?"

"Interrogation of this pilot."

"I must stay for if I do not…" Bennett cut him off.

"You are most welcome, Chungjwa. Please sit down." Chungjwa did so and glared at Carter. In a few brief words Bennett explained what the pilot had thus far revealed. Chungjwa showed genuine alarm when he heard that the Allies had got as far north as Seoul. Everything they had all been told up until now suggested that the Allies were as good as thrown into the sea on the far south coast.

"You believe him?" Bennett grinned cruelly.

"Men facing what he *thinks* he is facing tend to lean towards telling the truth." Bennett turned back to Carter.

"Who commands the force attacking Korea?"

Carter looked at Bennett in puzzlement.

"Attacking Korea, sir?"

"WHO COMMANDS?" Bennett shouted

Terrified, Carter stuttered, "General of the Army MacArthur, sir. He commands the Allies."

"And what countries make up the *Allies*?" Bennett said with sarcastic exaggeration of the last word.

"I don't know them all, sir, but many countries: United States, South Korea, Great Britain, Canada, Australia, New Zealand, France and many more... the United Nations."

"Gun," Earl handed the gun to Bennett.

Carter literally shook in fear. "No sir, please."

"If you are lying to me, *Lieutenant.*"

"I'm not lying sir, I swear!" Tears ran down his cheeks.

"Lock him up, away from the other."

As Gerard led the whimpering Carter away Bennett turned on Chungjwa and fixed him with a glare. As soon as the door shut on Carter and Gerard he switched back to English.

"You and Mr Moore in my quarters this instant."

The three men walked out across the corridor and into the officers' quarters, then down the long hall and at the end Bennett threw open his door and stepped aside for the other two to enter. As soon as they did he slammed the door and turned on Chungjwa.

"Did you know about this?"

Chungjwa looked hurt. "No, sir."

"Good God! Bennett exploded, "We come here to help your country at great personal risk. We stay here for years, then you ask for more and we fight *and die* to oblige against my better judgement, and all the while being told we are fighting the Americans and now we find out that not only are we fighting the whole bloody world but were fighting half the bloody country you claim we are here to protect! Jesus Christ, man!"

Chungjwa, utterly distraught, hung his head. "My part."

"What?"

"My part of the country, sir, my family, my friends, they are all from, and live in the south. Until now I didn't even know there was a north or south. Politically, yes but..."

"I see that, damn it."

As Moore looked at his commanding officer, he bore witness to a man quite literally tearing his hair out.

"God damn it." He composed himself, then let out a long sigh. When he spoke again his voice was calm. "I'm sorry, Chungjwa. He gave an ironic half smile and hissed, "My God, we have been led up the path here." Then suddenly a thought seemed to slap him in the face. "God what have I done… Price, Fitzsimmons, they died for a lie! My lie."

Moore cut in angrily but with pain and anguish all over his broad face.

"That's enough of that, sir. Allen, this was not your doing, not at all."

As if Moore hadn't spoken Bennett continued, "What the hell do we do now?"

"We make sure it's true," Moore snapped.

Bennett nodded and turned to Chungjwa. "Well, sir, if this is true our friends just became our enemies, which are you?"

Chungjwa straitened up and fixed Bennett with a meaningful stare. "Sir, be this true or untrue, I am your friend. But if it is true, I to have a new enemy. I will find out. The guards on rotation will know and they trust me. I will find out, sir, and I will come to you with what I find. I swear it."

"Very well. Until I hear otherwise I must assume this is true, and this being so, we are leaving. But I must decide how. For now however, not a whisper, not a hint we know any of this or we're all dead men. Earl, go and make sure Mr Gerard and Mr Metzger do not speak a word of what they just heard."

"It was terrible to see him like that, he was heartbroken, and it was plain to see, I'd seen it before when your uncle died."

"I'm still bitter you didn't see fit to talk to us," Hector mumbled but not angrily.

"What would we have told you? That we were in great peril and had no idea how to get out? That would have helped."

At this point Mother came in. "Right boys, it's time for lunch."

After lunch Hector made his excuses and decided to walk back to Peaslake and visit the pub, I decided to go with him that far and then go up to the wood to read more of my father's journal. I wanted to look at the thoughts Earl and Hector couldn't show me. As we walked out the garden gate Hector grinned.

"So, what are you making of all this, William?"

"Well, I knew my father and Earl had a colourful past, but I had no idea that it would be like this."

"No, you wouldn't, and nor would anybody else. That was the point."

"How many of you got home?" I asked without thinking.

"Wouldn't that be rather skipping pages?"

"Yes, of course. It's just that the more of this story I find out, the more starts to make sense."

Hector chuckled.

"Why did you go so far away? Yorkshire, I mean? When they were all here?"

"All?"

"Well, my father, Earl, Chungjwa…"

"He's here?" Hector asked in astonishment.

"Oh, I thought you knew."

Hector put on a broad smile and chuckled again. "No, I didn't, but I shouldn't have been surprised, he and your father were close. Not like Earl but… Well, I guess I thought he would have gone home by now. And he's here?"

"Yes, I've seen him at my father's grave a few times."

"Blimey, would be good to see the little bugger again."

"Ask at the inn, they might know where he lives?"

"I wouldn't mind betting Earl knows. What's in the satchel anyway?"

"Oh, nothing. Just a book and a few other bits and bobs." After we had walked a bit further in silence, I decided to ask a question that had been bugging me. "Hector, do you think my father was wrong to do what he did?"

He looked at me and paused in his walking.

"Well, that is not an easy question to answer. It depends from where you look at it. From the RAF's position, yes. It was effectively desertion, not to mention theft of His Majesties Aircraft. Not that they wouldn't have been scrapped anyway but that's not the point. From his pilot's point of view no, I don't think so. He gave us a choice and bore no ill will towards those who decided to go. As for the rest, it's simple. You can't blame a man for making a decision based on the lies of another. He and all of us were doing what we thought was right, but we trusted the people who told us we should and why. We couldn't know they were lying through their evil twisted teeth, could we? And the minute we did…"

"What, what did you do?"

"Well that would be skipping pages again." He said and grinned warmly. "Also of course we were all on the point of becoming unemployed. The war was over, what were we to do? Go back to the clerks and builders we'd been before? I think not. This couldn't have come at a better time. We wanted it to work out as much as your father. Anyway peace sounded so bloody boring" I smiled at him but I was troubled. As we reached Peaslake Hector chuckled in his usual way looking at the Inn. "Right, young lad, I'm off to sink a couple." And with that he walked off.

I readjusted my bag and began the climb up past the church. As I passed the graveyard I saw nobody and walked on deeper into the wood. The path was a wide, sand one, and as I was burning with anticipation I pulled out the journal and read as I walked. As before, I scanned through the pages looking for events of significance, unlike before, there were many. I knew what I was looking for though. I went back to where I had left off and only a page or two further on I found the report on the accidental combat on the 12th of June.

12th June 1950:1

D1	*S.L. Bennett*	*Kangaroo – Base One*	*T/O*	*08:47*
D6	*P.O. Sharpe*	*Kangaroo – Base One*	*T/O*	*08:47*
D7	*P.O. Fitzsimmons*	*Kangaroo – Base One*	*T/O*	*08:48*
D1	*S.L. Bennett*	*Return*	*L*	*17:11*
D6	*P.O. Sharpe*	*Return, Damaged*	*L*	*17:12*
D7	*P.O. Fitzsimmons*	*Shot Down, KIA*	*L*	****
D2	*F.L. Price*	*Scramble*	*T/O 16:20 – L 17:12*	
D3	*F.L. Fitzsimmons*	*Scramble*	*T/O 16:20 – L 17:12*	
D4	*O.L. Metzger*	*Scramble*	*T/O 16:20 – L 17:13*	
D5	*P.O. Quinn*	*Scramble*	*T/O 16:21 – L 17:13*	
D8	*F.S. Kilmartin*	*Scramble*	*T/O 16:21 – L17:14*	

It is with great sorrow, that I record the death of the first pilot since we came to this land. Made considerably worse by the fact we are now not only in a war zone, but we are now involved in war, rather than the intended position of training others to be involved, forced into this by tragic circumstance...

I read my father's description of the fight up until he closed the official diary for that day in the way he generally did. Then, as he generally did, he added his personal thoughts.

It eats at my soul that Timothy does not walk with us any longer, Even more so because were it not for my decisions, my orders, he still would be. Peace is not like war. In war things were simple, then peace came and the thought of it implied more of a life and death struggle than war ever did. The irony. In war, one can find peace, in peace, one looks for a war. I found a war, and were it just me I could live with it. But I brought war to others, and now they are dying. I don't know how I will ever live with that. I damn myself for this. But I damn the god damn bloody Yanks to a boiling fiery hell for this as well. The papers must have been right. They won't be satisfied until they rule the entire world. Do I continue to lose men in an attempt to stop them? Is that the right thing to do? Do we stand a chance?

My father was a man clearly on the edge of reason. Hurting, alone, scared, and working on information that, unbeknownst to him, was entirely false. How I wished I could have been there and leapt out the pages he was writing and told him how things really were. If only he had known. Again, I felt that keen feeling of loss. I missed him, I missed a man I never really knew. How I wished he had told me all this when he was alive. But it was too late.

Turning pages. I found repair reports, training flights, formation plans, battle tactics, meetings, briefings and then the next fight over Base One

14th July 1950:2

D1   S.L. Bennett   Intercept, Damaged   T/O 08:14 - L 09:41

D2	FL Price	Intercept	T/O 08 :14 - L 10:17
D3	FL Fitzsimmons	Intercept	T/O 08 :15 - L 09:48
D4	OL Metzger	Intercept, Damaged	T/O 08:15 - L 10:16
D5	PO Quinn	Intercept	T/O 08:15 - L 09:42
D6	PO Sharpe	Intercept	T/O 08:15 - L 09:49
D8	FS Kilmartin	Intercept, Damaged	T/O 08:16 - L 09:49

Mission Assignment: Intercept

Again, I read my father's words that described in graphic detail the action over Base One In every line I detected fear, but never for himself, only for his men.

My God, that was a hot fight. I only praise him that we lost nobody, a fact I can only believe, is due to the incredible flying skill and talent of the extraordinary men I have the honour of commanding. Three damaged, myself included! It could so easily have been three lost. I would give my life a thousand times over if only it meant I could get these men out of here safely and give them the peace they so deserve.

At this point I walked squarely into a tree, banging my head hard on a branch and dropped the journal. Rubbing my head and cursing my own stupidity, I picked up the journal and realised I had walked clear past the place where I had intended to sit down. Turning to walk back I suddenly noticed a small piece of paper had fallen out of the journal when it dropped. I picked it up but it was not a piece of paper but an envelope with a hand written letter inside. I stood, considering. This could be anything, from anybody to anybody but it could also tell me something it was not time for me to know. I resolved to read it when I knew more. Putting it in the side pocket of the satchel, I walked back to where I had intended and sat down overlooking a splendid scene. The land stretched away for miles and miles. This was my land, my home. What must my father have thought in Korea when he looked out on such a scene far from his true home? Could he have felt like I do? I thought not. Were I him, I would have always felt like a part of me was missing, that I did not belong.

15ᵗʰ July 1950:3

D1	*SL Bennett*	*Intercept*	*T/O, 09:22 - L 10:16*
D2	*FL Price*	*Intercept*	*T/O, 09:22 - L 10:17*
D3	*FL Fitzimmons*	*Intercept*	*T/O, 09:23 - L 10:18*
D9	*OL Metzger*	*Intercept*	*T/O, 09:23 - L 10:18*
D5	*PO Quinn*	*Intercept*	*T/O, 09:23 - L 10:19*
D6	*PO Sharpe*	*Intercept*	*T/O, 09:24 - L 10:20*
D11	*FS Kilmartin*	*Intercept*	*T/O, 09:24 - L 10:22*

Mission Assignment: Intercept

What a day. These new-fangled jets are nothing like I expected. We can't outrun them, we can't out climb them, its almost impossible to give chase to them, but by God, we can out turn them. They are so fast they can't follow, and all the time that is the case, we have no cause to fear them. Not only that, but they carry so much fuel that a good burst of our cannon and they are lost. I am so relieved. I thought that things had moved on to such a degree that we would be left behind, our tactics obsolete. It would seem that this is further in the future than I thought.

As I read this I couldn't help but feel there was a ring of panic in his words. Having read what I had, it seemed like he was swinging from moments of extreme anguish and depression regarding his situation, to feeling delirious with heartfelt relief the next. Literally from one report to another. Then it came, the report I had been fearing:

20th August 1950:4

D1	*SL Bennett*	*Intercept*	*T/O 08:14 - L 09:41*
D2	*FL Price*	*Intercept, Shot Down, KIA*	*T/O 08 :14 - L*****
D3	*FL Fitzsimmons*	*Intercept, Damaged*	*T/O 08:15 - L 09:48*
D4	*OL Metzger*	*Intercept*	*T/O 08:15 - L 10:16*
D5	*PO Quinn*	*Intercept, Damaged*	*T/O 08:15 - L 09:42*
D6	*PO Sharpe*	*Intercept, Shot Down, Crashed*	*T/O 08:15 - L *****

Mission Assignment: Intercept

There was nothing, no notation, no mission description, no personal thoughts. I guess he just couldn't do it, but it was clear that he was a man falling apart under the weight of his own torment. Not only that, but over the next few weeks there was very little comment at all. Then the reports returned but the personal comments remained absent. Then came the reports and comments of the missions that had tried and failed to find a target and again I found examples of a man torn between fear of losing those he wished to save and raw hatred of those he wished to bring down.

Scramble drills continue. The lads are still making good time, two minutes by day, just over three by night.

Three times now we have been up to search for an enemy we knew was there, yet could not find. They hide in the cloud cover, or else they are so fast that by the time we get to the location they are long gone with no chance of catching them up. It is more than I can bear. If we find them we might kill them, they might kill us. If we don't we all live and the war goes on with no end in sight and no damage done to the enemy. I'm tired, I'm so tired, sick and tired! I need to be free of this life and death struggle. I need to be free of this life.

It was hard to see my father's thoughts in this way, the pages betraying what he had spent a lifetime trying to hide. Again, I found myself wondering why he had kept this journal. It made no sense, he had no orders to, no need to, and the very fact that it existed put both him and his men in deadly peril if found by the wrong people. It could have just been to keep him busy I supposed, but if that were the case, why not destroy it when he got out, why take it with him?

After flicking through more pages containing nothing much, I found the day when Hector had returned to duty and a brief comment from my father to the effect that he was relieved. Then as I began to get toward the point where Earl had left off, I got to what I assumed was their last combat.

01st October 1950:5

D1	S.L. Bennett	Kangaroo- Base One	T/O, 08:14
D3	F.L. Fitzsimmons	Kangaroo- Base One	T/O, 08 :15
D4	O.L. Metzger	Kangaroo- Base One	T/O, 08:15
D5	P.O. Quinn	Kangaroo- Base One	T/O, 08:15
D9	P.O. Sharpe	Kangaroo- Base One	T/O, 08:15
D8	F.S. Kilmartin	Kangaroo- Base One	T/O, 08:16
D1	S.L. Bennett	Return	L, 15:49
D3	F.L. Fitzsimmons	Return	L, 15:51
D4	O.L. Metzger	Return	L, 15:53
D5	P.O. Quinn	Return	L, 15:30
D9	P.O. Sharpe	Return	L, 15:55

D8   F.S. Kilmartin   *Return*   L, 15:57

To my surprise, there was nothing else written. When I turned the page, the routine reports began again. This time even more minimal than they had been since the day Mr Price had been killed. Burning with curiosity, I put the journal back in my bag and headed home at a brisk walk to speak to Earl. As I walked through Peaslake my eye fell on the Inn and I walked in. It was loud inside. The area by the bar busy. Seeing no sign of Hector, I went up to the bar and hailed the barman who was the father of a friend.

"Is Hector Sharpe here, Tony? The one staying?"

"No, William, he met up with some fella then left."

"Thanks."

I walked back out and continued home. Now, who on earth would Hector be meeting here? Not Earl, he was still housebound.

As I walked through the door I heard Hector's laugh from the lounge and walked through to be greeted by the sight of Mother, Earl, Hector and Chungjwa all sat around and talking as if family. For a split second, unlike all the times I had been around with Earl or Hector up till now, Mother was not stiff and formal as she usually was, but relaxed, she even seemed to be enjoying herself. There was something here I clearly had yet to understand. They had all fallen quiet on hearing somebody approach, but as I walked in Chungjwa shot to his feet and bowed. Hector laughed again.

"Oh loosen up, old fellow. Hello, William, we are all here, as you see. Come in, sit down." Hector boomed.

"Would anybody like some tea?" Mother quickly asked.

"Tea be damned, my lovely, it's too late in the day for tea. Beer my lovely. Beer."

"I'd say you have had one to many of those already, wouldn't you?" Earl put in with a hint of warning in his voice.

"There is no such circumstance," Hector said beaming.

"Very well," Mother sighed. But not angrily, and with great dignity, rose and left the room.

"So, this is who you found in the inn?" I asked Hector.

"Yes indeed, my old comrade in arms, and by a long way, senior to us all. Yet he acts as if he is the merest servant." Hector chuckled, patting Chungjwa affectionately on the shoulder.

"Enough Hector," Earl said with an air of impatience. "Have a seat, Will."

I sat down and Earl put on a thin and friendly smile.

"So, Will, whilst this has been a bit premature and unplanned these two walked in and now seems a very good opportunity to talk about what happened next in your father's story. Chungjwa knows what is going on and like Hector is happy to tell you what he knows."

I glanced at Chungjwa, who bowed his head and smiled. The first smile I had ever seen from him.

"Are you up to date on your father's thoughts?" Earl asked knowingly.

"Not entirely."

Earl gave me a questioning look.

"I read up to the last fight when you took prisoners but there was nothing from that moment on."

"What do you mean, read?" Hector asked, leaning forward in sudden interest with a look of alarm. "Tell them, Will."

"My father kept a squadron diary, well, a squadron and personal diary if you like." Hector's look of alarm grew.

"He what?"

Earl quickly cut in. "It's safe Hector, it always has been, and always will be."

"For Christ's sake." Hector exploded in sudden anger. "That bloody book could have us behind bars for the rest of our bloody lives, or worse!"

"Calm down, Hector." Earl growled. "It's safe."

Visibly controlling his anger, Hector leaned back in his chair with a muttered comment inaudible to all.

"You say there is nothing after the day we shot down those two, well there wouldn't be." Pausing and looking at the others. "Our base was full of spies working for the Soviets and North Koreans."

"Yes, that snivelling weasel of the guard commander for one," Hector spat.

"Indeed. Your father knew this and it was not impossible that that journal could be found. Everything changed that night, and had the authorities got wind of it they might have had us all shot. No doubt your father knew this and took precautions."

"So, what did happen?"
"Well as I told you before, Chungjwa was sent to find out the truth of the matter, with us happy that if he found anything he would tell us."

"So, what did you find?" I asked turning to Chungjwa but Earl answered for him.

"Before we get to that…"

Chapter 11

The Truth

Squadron Leader Bennett, looking drawn and tired, was sat at his desk writing. It was now late and the base was quiet. It had been hours since they had interrogated Carter and McKinnon but Bennett had plenty to do. Despite this, he was working at half speed whilst the torment of his inner feelings clawed at him. Suddenly the door flew open without a knock and Pamez stormed in.

"Major," Bennett said coldly, his body and features not moving one inch.

"It is customary to knock when entering a commanding officers' quarters."

"You have prisoners?" Pamez asked with a look of venom. Bennett shot to his feel and glared at Pamez.

"You call me, sir, damnit, *Major,* and don't take that tone with me. I command here."

"You have prisoners… sir?"

Bennett sat back down and smiled as if his last outburst had never happened. "I do, a sorry bunch of lying scheming scum but I have two."

"I am here to take them to headquarters for questioning."

"Very well. I fancy you will want this. Bennett handed over the document he had been writing. Pamez took it.

"What is this… sir?"

"A record of the interrogation I have already made. All lies, of course, but for what it's worth, you should know that they believe us to be Korean, so I would be much obliged if we could talk in just that language"

Pamez nodded sharply and Bennett rose and walked from the room with Pamez close behind. Walking through corridors, they reached the guard room where Bennett instructed the prisoners to be released into the Major's care.

"Do you require a guard for them?"

"That will not be necessary." Bennett's eyebrows angled and he glared at Pamez who grudgingly added. "Sir."

The two Americans emerged from two different sides. Seeing each other, Carter stared in amazement at the patched-up figure of his senior who had clearly not suffered at all at the hands of their captors and in fact, had been bandaged and cleaned up. Realisation dawned and he hung his head.

Seeing this MacKinnon barked, "What did you tell them, Lieutenant?"

"Silence!" Pamez snapped in English and drew a pistol. "Move."

The group moved down the corridor and eventually entered the hangar where Bennett saw a small group of soldiers waiting in a row, and on seeing them the group advanced and stood on either side of the prisoners.

"Good night, sir," Pamez growled in fast Korean and began to walk towards the exit. At this point. Mackinnon wheeled on Carter.

"What did you tell them you little pipsqueak?"

"Silence," Pamez snapped again.

"Fuck you," Mackinnon spat and wheeled again on Carter who looked very sheepish indeed. A shot rang out and reverberated round the hangar, magnifying the sound tenfold. The bullet entered the back of Mackinnon's head and as it exited through the face, shattering it into a congealed mess of muscle and broken bone, a significant portion was splattered all over Carter's face. Carter let out a small squeak and collapsed. Bennett, who had turned to walk back into the central corridor, now stopped and slowly turned to Pamez with a look of burning rage written over every inch of his face which quickly turned red. Holding his glare he finally spoke.

"Major Pamez, take yourself and your men and that idiot," pointing at Carter, "and get the fuck… off my base."

Pamez turned and stalked away, his men dragging the limp body of Carter behind. Finally, the small door in the main hangar door slammed shut and Moore stepped out of the shadows. "That man is an animal. I've seen his kind before, in Germany."

"Yes, he is, and so have I. I hoped I would never fight on the same side as such a one."

"You always have, sir, but at least now we have a choice." At this moment, Chungjwa walked in. Seeing the body, he stopped short. Pulling himself together he walked up to Bennett and whispered, "I need to speak to you sir, now."

"My quarters, Earl, if you would."

The three men left the hangar and went to Bennett's room. As soon as they were inside, Earl closed the door and locked it.

Turning to his CO he said, "Sir, did you really tell Pamez what the Yanks said?"

"A very watered down and a lot less plausible version of it, yes. If I hadn't he would only have extracted the truth from Carter later. Besides, I have a feeling that the unfortunate lieutenant is not long for this world anyway."

"Sir," Chungjwa said, "I must tell you what I know."

"Go on."

"Sir, Carter was telling the truth, all of it. And there's more. Your men, they're all dead."

"What the devil do you mean?"

"The men that left when you first arrived, they're all dead, killed by the authorities to stop them passing on information about what was going on."

Bennett sank into a chair. He fixed a withering look on Chungjwa. "How do you know this?"

"I listened, and when the time was right I put a lot of drink in the right places. That, and I have my own spies that I put to work."

"What else?"

"The allied forces were almost pushed into the sea last month, but now they have fought back in much greater numbers and better supported, they are half way up the country now with little chance of holding them. The lines have stopped where they apparently first began. Nobody knows if they will continue north or not, but neither my contacts nor I can think of any reason why they should not. They could be here in weeks, possibly less."

Bennett leaned his elbows on his desk and sank his head into his hands. After a long pause he finally spoke. "That's it then, we are leaving. Earl, where are we with a plan?"

"Well, sir, we have a plan but with no guarantee. Should I get Mr Fitzsimmons and go over it?"

"Very well."

Minutes later saw Fitzsimmons join the three. They all sat down in the cramped space.

"So, gentlemen," Bennett said in almost a whisper.

"What have you got?" Fitzsimmons spoke.

"Sir, we are working on old intelligence and estimated numbers, however, here are the figures as best we can estimate. The Dakota, with its extra fuel capacity, is capable of approximately two thousand four hundred miles. The Tempests, significantly less than half that, even with tanks. There is no friendly territory to the west, north west, north, north east. To the east we have nothing but islands of Japan and a big pond they call the Pacific. To the south east, Japan, held, as far as we know, by the Americans. Americans that will ask a lot of questions if *we* suddenly appear. To the south, the East China Sea and beyond that, the Philippines, again held by the US but far enough away that questions may be a little more friendly. To the south west, Hong Kong, held by the British and as such will be laden with a lot of questions at the end of which, a long sentence behind bars possibly worse. So, it must be south. Land in the Philippines, demand a refuel. Then on."

"On to where?"

"Australia."

"Australia?"

"We believe it is our only option. Pick up a ship and go home."

"That all sounds far too simple!"

"Indeed, we need an escort, we will never get out of this war zone without one. We can't guarantee a refuel, without which we have no hope. If we get to Australia, we have no guarantee that we will be able to get a ship to England, and if we get to England, we have no guarantee that we will be able to hide in a way that will let us live the rest of our lives in peace. However, we have explored all possible options, believe me and this is the best we can come up with. All others are fraught with even less desirable uncertainties."

"Very well, if that's what you think. Let's have all pilots in the operations room in thirty minutes. Do it quietly and do not be seen by the guards."

Chungjwa cut in.

"Most of the internal staff are asleep, the guard outside won't be changed till tomorrow morning. And the head of the guard has had enough to keep him asleep for some time."

"I'll start waking them up," Moore said. "I think Mr Sharpe and Mr Kilmartin are still in the bar."

"Right, gentlemen, I need this kept quiet, and we must move swiftly." The bleary-eyed pilots looked on in concern, knowing that whatever was coming must be of grave significance to have them hoisted out of bed. "Right, we are leaving, all of us. From intelligence gained from the Americans we shot down earlier is has become clear that we have been lied to. I won't go over the details now because there is too much to do but suffice to say, we must leave as soon as it can be arranged. Mr Fitzsimmons and Mr Moore, under my instructions, have been working on a plan for some time to extract us in the event it became necessary and I will ask them now to brief you." Fitzsimmons stood up.

"Right, gentlemen, as you will know, the Dakota is fully fuelled and has been for some time. Tomorrow night, after the internal guard are asleep at around three a.m., Chungjwa and Mr Sharpe will be taking members of the external guard for a quick walk from which they will not return. We must get the Dakota and all the ground crew onto the strip and be ready to roll at a moment's notice. Mr Quinn will be pilot, with Mr Kilmartin alongside. Squadron Leader Bennett, Mr Metzger and myself will be in D1, D4 and I will be in NV952. We will get into the air as swiftly as we can heading west south west until we reach the Yellow Sea. We then turn south out of sight of land and remain on a straight southerly course for just over one thousand miles when we should raise the Philippine islands. There we will land at the first airbase we find, of which there are many, refuel and take off again headed south again, over the islands of Borneo to its east and Indonesia and then to the north coast of Australia where we will land and find a ship back to Britain."

Quin's voice cut in. "I won't ask why we are leaving for now, but I do want to point out that as we all know the Tempests don't have anything like that range so...?"

Fitzsimmons gave a mischievous smile.

"Quite right, Mr Quinn. On this we have no choice. We can't get out of this war zone without an escort. D1 and D4 will have Korean colours but the Dakota and NV952 will have British. It is our hope that if we meet with Soviet aircraft, D1 and D4 will wave them off. If we meet allied aircraft, I will do likewise. But if this doesn't work then we will have to fight it out and, at all costs, we will protect the Dakota. In aid of further protection, we will be mounting two guns facing to port and starboard of the Dakota manned by Mr Sharpe and Mr Gerard. When the Tempests run out of fuel we should be well away and one by one we will hoist the pilots into the Dakota."

"What!" Metzger's voice cut in as he shot to his feet. "Hoist in?!"

"We will stream out a line from the rear door of the Dakota, each aircraft in turn will approach, canopy open and link the line to their parachute harness, jump clear and be pulled in by the men on the Dakota."

Metzger looked on appalled. "Jesus," he said with a sigh, and looking dazed collapsed back into his chair.

"Gentlemen, I'm not saying this plan is perfect, but it is all we have after weeks of work, and believe me when I tell you, it is essential we leave as soon as it can be done," Bennett said.

"Overall command of the fight will rest with Mr Moore; his word is final." Moore shot Bennett a glance of surprise and then quickly re-arranged his features in to one of knowing calm.

"Metzger wasn't happy but after talking through the alternatives, he resigned himself to the idea that there was no other way. The others seemed resigned to the idea and trusted there was a good reason for it."

"When was this?" Earl looked at me questioningly.

"Well, I don't remember the date exactly but late the same night we shot down the American fighter. Why?"

Reaching for my satchel I pulled out the journal. Hector leaned forward and looked enquiringly at the journal. Turning the pages, I soon found it. "Here, second of October."

Mission 6

03ʳᵈᵗʰ October 1950:6

D1	**SL Bennett**	**Escort**	**T/O, 03:40**
NV952	**FL Fitzsimmons**	**Escort**	**T/O, 03:40**
D4	**OL Metzger**	**Escort**	**T/O, 03:40**
44-76382	**PO Quinn**	**Transport**	**T/O, 03:39**
	FS Kilmartin		
	WC Lee Jung Soon		
	FL Moore		
	FO Gerard		
	PO Sharpe		
	WO Morgan		
	Cpl Squires		
	LAC Lawrence		
	LAC Taylor		
	LAC Dean		
	AC Adaway		

Mission Assignment: Escape!

I deliberately didn't read the entry and turned back to Earl.
"So, did it work?" Earl gave a grunt and a half smile.

"Yes and no. We knew we couldn't open the hangar doors without waking up the guard so I concocted a fault in one aircraft and decided to test them all which meant running them for half an hour. We couldn't do this inside ya see so we got D1, D4 and NV952 out to test them in the assembly area as it was getting dark and the chances of being seen were passed. Then your father loudly declared the aircraft should be left out until first light as he wanted the hangar doors closed. So that night, as planned, the internal guard went to bed, the external guard of six went off with Chungjwa and Hector and…"

"What did you do?" I said, looking at Hector. I knew it was a stupid question but it had just come out. Hector looked passively at the ceiling and leaned back in his chair.

"Well it's the strangest thing. They simply vanished. One minute they were there, then poof." Rolling my eyes to the heavens and looking back at Earl.

"Sorry, Earl, you were saying?" Earl looked at me with infinite patience.

"The DC3 had been checked and rechecked and all the camouflage removed. A short time passed and then, with your father's permission, the order was given to start all engines and go."

In moonlit darkness three Tempests sat silent, pulled into line by hand behind a Dakota at the head of the strip. Not a sound was heard and nothing moved. Beside the Dakotas open rear doors Squadron Leader Bennett and Flight Lieutenant Moore stood surveying the scene. Warrant Officer Morgan loomed up out of the darkness and nodded at Moore.

"Four minutes sir."

Moore turned to Bennett who grinned and said.

"Let's go, and briskly I think"

"Yes, sir." Moore held up his arm torch in hand and in seconds, five engines roared into life. Earl sprinted to the doors of the Dakota as Bennett ran for his Tempest. Only seconds passed as one by one the aircraft hurtled down the strip and into the darkness.

"Delta 1 to all aircraft assume positions."

Climbing as fast as its heavily loaded frame would allow the Dakota clawed for height as the Tempests climbed high above. Less than a minute after the last Tempest had taken off a blinding flash and huge roaring explosion split the night. Feeling the shock of the concussion Bennett in Delta 1 looked back to see what was left of Kangaroo airbase erupt into a sea of flame and falling rock. Then subside once more into darkness as the hillside gave way burying for ever the last base he would ever command. The radio remained silent. Nobody could think of anything to say.

Minutes later Quinn reached three thousand feet and levelled off. Three thousand feet above him D1, NV952 and D4 levelled off and scanned the skies. But in the darkness, even if there had been something there, there was no chance they would see it. Steadily they worked their way across land; aboard the Dakota all eyes scanned for aircraft, but like the fighters with no result. Sharpe walked forward and up to Moore, shouting over the noise of the aircrafts two huge radial engines. "Nothing in sight, Earl. Soon we should be clear."

"Clear be damned," Earl shouted back. "They're out there. Have those guns ready."

Sharpe grinned. "Yes sir."

As the first light of dawn crept over the horizon and the Yellow Sea sprawled before them, a cry shattered the peace.

"Bandits, six o'clock, high."

Bennett had seen them at the same moment from above.

"Delta 1 to all aircraft, I know those markings, it's Pamez, dive and engage."

As the four Soviet, and two Korean aircraft closed with the Dakota they clearly had no idea that far above, three Tempests were diving towards them. At the last moment the lead aircraft broke off as the Tempests roared down. Cannon fire split the sky and two Yaks were hit. One lost a wingtip and its pilot grappled for control, the other dived as its engine seized and also descended out of the fight. Machine gun fire rattled out from the port side of the Dakota, striking hits on another but with no effect. A Yak with Korean markings made an attempt to turn behind the Dakota but Metzger was ready, and, having pulled hard up after his first attack, rolled over slowing as he did so and his aircraft spat forty explosive rounds a second out of its four 20mm cannon. He could not miss. The aircraft shuddered as the cannon shells tore parts away. The cockpit shattered and the Yak ceased manoeuvring, flying off into the morning light. But Metzger had failed to notice Major Pamez, who, seeing that he was going after another, had turned hard to starboard and opened a long burst of fire as Metzger crossed in front of him. Metzger's Tempest shook as rounds hammered into it. One punched through the cockpit wall and hit Metzger's left arm. Blood pulsed. Another hit him in the chest and Metzger coughed with the impact. Bennett, watching, came around and fired a long burst at Pamez, but though his aircraft was hit it continued to manoeuvre furiously.

"V, on your tail," Bennett shouted and Fitzsimmons put flaps down and pulled hard back as his aircraft almost stopped in mid-air.

Stalling, the Tempest now fell from the sky as Bennett dived down again to engage. His cannon rang out and a flash in the sky indicated that the Yak he had fired at had been heavily hit and now fell to earth a shattered wreck. Fitzsimmons regained control and pulled hard up. Directly in front of him a Soviet Yak was making an attack on the Dakota but even as he watched, the Dakota fired into the attacker and the enemy ceased fire and flew away.

Battered and bleeding, Metzger tried to circle around to engage the aircraft that had hit him. Firing a long burst, he missed and his guns fell silent.

"Delta 4," he wheezed in pain coughing up blood. "I'm out."

Fitzsimmons was trying to catch up and Bennett was far below as Pamez rolled and dived on the Dakota. Opening fire, machine gun bullets struck the cockpit and Kilmartin shuddered as a bullet split his skull and he fell limp over the controls. Then a huge explosion shook the Dakota again as Metzger's Tempest ploughed squarely into Pamez's Yak and the burning and twisted remanence of the two aircraft plummeted down into the dark ocean below. Silence rained once more. Bennett had been watching helplessly and gave an involuntary sob. Then he ground his teeth.

"Delta 1 to all aircraft, keep your eyes peeled, some of those bastards might be back. I'm sorry to say we have lost Delta 4." Quinn's voice crackled.

"Skip, I'm sorry to say we have lost Mr Kilmartin too. Mr Sharpe has replaced him, and Mr Morgan now has starboard gun."

Trying to keep his voice from betraying his anguish Bennett simply replied, "Thank you."

Minutes later, the flight set course south and began their run down the Yellow Sea headed for the East China Sea. After an hour on their southward course, Moor's voice crackled over the radio.

"Transport to Delta 1, sir, we are now south of the battle line. I submit it is wise to bring you aboard now."

"Delta 1 to transport, if that is what you have decided?"

"Assume the position and hold."

"Delta 1, roger."

Bennett descended and formatted on the Dakota. Very slowly he inched his way below and just behind the port main door. The door opened, and a heavy line, weighted with a lump of metal, began to slowly trail behind and towards Bennett. Morgan's customary bravado had vanished as he looked on in horror at the aircraft that was so close that one false move would have them all in the sea. Only feet away was the Tempest's huge propeller; if the line went into that they were in serious trouble too. Suddenly the line entered the propeller turbulence of the Tempest and took to bouncing up and down making it even harder. For minutes the line flew up and down sometimes, striking the Tempests and sometimes missing altogether. Giving up on getting the line into the cockpit, Bennett descended out of the line's reach, and jettisoned the canopy all together. Then he came up again for another try. Holding out a hand he suddenly grasped the line. Pre-prepared with a clip, he latched it quickly over his parachute harness and, releasing his belt straps that held him to his aircraft, he pulled the throttle right back and shoved the yoke hard forward. The Tempest dove away. In an instant, Bennett was snatched out of his cockpit and warned by Morgan, the Dakota turned hard to starboard and climbed to get away from the now unmanned and uncontrollable Delta 1. With all the strength they could muster, Morgan, Squires, Tayleur and Adaway heaved Bennett up. Finally getting him to the door, Moore reached out and grabbed his friend by the hand, helping him in. The door slammed shut once more and the deafening noise of wind rush ceased.

"Jesus," Bennett said panting madly. "I wouldn't want to do that again."

Gazing out the window he watched as his faithful Tempest curved away very slowly to port and finally fell away out of sight. Moore hung back respectfully understanding the pang of sadness this must have brought.

Finally, Bennett straightened and, noticing everybody staring at him, shouted over the noise. "This isn't a bloody freak show, get your damned eyes out there," he said, stabbing a finger at the nearest window "Not in here!"

Quickly scattering, everybody found a window to look out of except Chungjwa who walked up to Bennett and warmly shook his hand with a smile.

"Honoured you could join us, sir," he said, meaning every word. Bennett allowed a ghost of a smile and gestured that they should move forward. Trying not to look at the covered body of Kilmartin as he passed it they reached the cockpit where Bennett shook Quinn's hand.

"Hot work, sir."

"Damned cold, actually," Bennett corrected with a smile. "May I?" Bennett said, holding out his hand to Sharpe and gesturing at his head set. Quickly removing his earphones Bennett put them on. "Delta 1, signing off Mr Fitzsimmons." A laugh came over the radio. "Well done skip I'm back above at six thousand."

"Roger, word of advice, when your turn comes, jettison your canopy before you approach."

"Roger, skip."

More time passed but nothing was seen. Finally, Sharpe turned to Bennett. "Sir, by my best calculations we should be flying off the southern most point of Korea now. We have Shanghai to the west and Japan to the East."

"Very well," Bennett said, and gestured for the headphones again.

"Transport to Escort, what is your fuel state?"

"Escort to Transport, I've got another couple of hundred miles in me."

"Transport to Escort, not necessary, we will get you aboard."

"Roger, skip, on my way." As Bennett had, Fitzsimmons dropped into position, jettisoning his canopy as he did so.

To Bennett's huge relief, Fitzsimmons was hauled in minutes later, and with a grin from ear to ear he staggered over.

"Piece of cake, don't know why it took you so long."

Bennett returned the smile. Then turned and returned to the cockpit. Reaching it he tapped Quinn on the shoulder and pointed downwards. Quinn nodded. The Dakota immediately began a slow descent finally levelling off at a mere three hundred feet.

"So, you got away?"

"Well I'd say it's fairly self-evident that we did, seeing as we are sat here," Hector said with a grin.

"Aye, we got away. Well, most of us did. Somewhere over the East China Sea we wrapped Kilmartin's body in a tarpaulin weighted with an ammunition box and tied together. Your father said a few words and Quinn dropped the DC3 down to one hundred where we opened the doors and, I guess you could say, committed his body to the deep. It was a hard decision for your father but we could hardly land at an airfield we didn't know with a body aboard and just hope nobody asked questions. It would be hard enough explaining the bullet damage!"

Earl sighed again and his eyes were locked on some part of the table in front of him. Then, pulling himself together, he broke the stare and looked back at me with that caring, withered expression.

"By George, it was a long flight though. Quinn was exhausted by the time we eventually sighted the Philippine islands."

"How did that go?" I asked bursting with curiosity.

"There," Sharpe suddenly shouted, pointing to his one o'clock. "That's an airfield or I'm a dutchman."

"Suits me!" muttered Quinn. Then more formally, "Mr Sharpe, shut down the port engine and feather prop."

"Roger, shutting down port engine, feathering prop." On one engine the Dakota descended and approached the runway.

"Gear down," Quinn ordered. Minutes later the wheels kissed the runway and the Dakota gracefully slowed. In stark contrast to the country they had left, it was a hot sunny day, although there had clearly been a good deal of rain lately, as static water could be seen everywhere. Splashing through a large puddle, the Dakota swung off the runway and came to a holt on the hardstand. Quinn shut down the starboard engine and sighed deeply. He turned to Bennett.

"Good luck, sir."

In the first silence in hours, Bennett raised his voice so all could hear. "I suggest, gentlemen, that you stretch your legs. You know what to do."

Adaway opened the doors and Bennett jumped down with Moore close behind. As they did so a jeep drove up with a man in engineers overalls at the wheel. Bennett walked up to him and said nervously, "Do you speak English?"

The man smiled and gestured for Bennett to get in. Bennett looked at Moore. "Clearly not. I think we better go with him." Moore nodded, and they both got in the van which swung round and drove towards a large hangar. Stopping outside their driver got out and gestured them to follow. Bennett and Moore got out and followed the little man into a small building beside the hangar where they found themselves standing in a recreation room. Another engineer was sat on a chair reading a newspaper but on noticing them enter he looked up. This was no Pilipino.

"Do you speak English?" Bennett asked again.

"I should do," the man replied with a smile. "Coming as I do... from Hampshire." Somewhat taken aback Bennett straightened.

"Squadron Leader Bennett, Flight Lieutenant Moore. Is there a base commander here?"

"Job, Marcus Job, sir ,and no, this is not a military base but a civil one. Though how, as a RAF man, you aren't aware of that is beyond me."

"Sir, we are a military transport from Hong Kong to Borneo transporting ex-prisoners of war from Korea home but we developed a fuel leak and had to divert here. We need fuel and an hour or so whilst my engineer handles the problem, will that be possible?"

"Um well now…"

"I understand there may be some expenses associated with landing here for an hour or so but my mission is too important to be held here long. Can I leave this with you to sort that and we will wait for the fuel at the aircraft?" As he said this Bennett drew out a large wad of dollar notes and placed them on the table.

Job's face widened in astonishment and a flicker of a smile showed. "I'm sure we can handle the paperwork, sir. Don't worry and given this could be considered something in the nature of an emergency then I will sort the fuel."

"Thank you, sir. Oh, there is one more thing," Bennett said, as casually as he could. "We were supposed to have some charts picked up at Hong Kong with details for flying on to Darwin after Borneo, but our idiot of a co-pilot forgot to collect them, do you have any here that might help us?"

"Darwin?" Job asked in surprise. "Well, yes, I can get you some charts."

"My thanks. Will your man take me back to my aircraft?"

"I'll take you myself." Barking orders in a language Bennett didn't understand Job got to his feet, snatched up the notes and, beaconing them to follow walked out.

Back at the hardstand Job looked up at the port wing on which Morgan and Adaway were making a pretence of working. "Do you need any help with that, sir?"

"I thank you, sir but there is no need. My boys know their business well. But I will be sure to come and find you if we do."

"Righto, well, I will leave you gentlemen, your fuel should be here very soon."

"Thank you for your help," Bennett said reverently.

"My pleasure sir, my pleasure, and if you need anything you just need to ask."

As Job drove away, a large truck detached itself from an area behind the hangar and headed straight for them. As it pulled up on the hardstand two men descended and began running out a hose from the back. Clearly both locals they said not a word as they fuelled the Dakota and when they were done they rolled up the hose and left as silently as they had come. Quinn, watching in amusement, turned to Bennett.

"Well I never, this is all a bit easy, we must have damn near emptied that bowser. I had the boys pumping it out of the tanks inside as they were pumping it in." He laughed.

"Long may it last," Bennett added coldly. Then more warmly he said, "You look tired, Mr Fitzsimmons and myself will take us the next leg."

"No argument here, sir," Quinn said with a grin then nodded at the hangar. "Here comes that chap again." Job drove up and smiled.

"All the paperwork's done, sir, so as soon as you're done with your work you're good to go, as they say, and here is the map you asked for."

"Thank you, we are done already. Mr Quinn, would you take this map to the cockpit?" Turning back to Job "Should we get permission from the tower to leave or…?"

"Lord bless you, no sir, you go ahead and roll out when you're ready. Just keep an eye out in case we get some more unexpected guests."

"Very well and thank you again."

"Have a safe trip, sir."

On board once more, Bennett quite literally ran up to the cockpit firmly, telling anybody listening to shut the door. He dropped into the pilot's seat and turned to Fitzsimmons.

"Ready?"

"And waiting, sir," Fitzsimmons replied with a smile. First one then the other engine turned over and fired and only minutes later they were rolling down the runway, building speed rapidly.

"It was that easy?" Earl smiled.

"Well, the flight as a whole no, but the deception, well, it was."

"I couldn't believe it either," Hector put in. "Dozy lot."

"So you flew to Darwin."

"We did." Earl looked at me for so long I began to worry. Then he spoke. "It was... Well, it was almost more than I could handle." Neither Hector or Chungjwa said a word.

"What?" I asked as if it would push Earl in to saying whatever he was thinking. Pain was written over every inch of his face, maybe not pain, despair.

Clearly knowing what was going through his mind Chungjwa spoke. "We had lost... Many... Good... friends." Suddenly Earl let loose a sob and to my surprise and dismay I turned back to him and saw his eyes redden and fill.

With all his humour gone Hector spoke, coldly.

"William, the world had changed, the war was over as far as anybody was concerned. But to us the war had only just ended, and only then were we able to look around and truly realise what we had lost. But worse than that, we realised that what we had lost.... needn't have been. Fitzsimmons, Price, Metzger, they hadn't died for a war and a great cause, they had died for nothing... nothing but us. And if that makes *us* hurt, think what it had done to your father."

I thought for a minute. Then I sat bolt upright as my brain bombarded me with a barrage of thoughts and strands of ideas. My father had lost the will to live. He feared peace more than he feared war, and to his men and I dare say his family, he was good at covering his inner torment. It was a tenuous link but, was the crash that killed my father really an accident?

"A good deal," a voice suddenly cut in. "More than you will, or would want to ever know." It was my mother, standing in the doorway looking on, and apparently for some time. "It destroyed him, every day and every night. From the first day I met him."

They had been in the air for hours. No longer afraid of detection they were cruising at ten thousand feet. Island after island had passed under them. On two occasions other aircraft had been sighted but had flown on not taking any notice of the lone transport. Having enjoyed a long sleep, Quinn had awoken and devoted much time to navigation, studying the chart they had acquired intently. Approaching the cockpit, he tapped Bennett on the shoulder. Bennett turned.

"Sir, I've been running the numbers. If we don't get a move on we may well reach Darwin in darkness."

The implications of this were severe and everyone in the cockpit knew it. Having crossed the Equator, they had moved from winter to summer but none the less, in darkness approaching an airstrip by eye was an almost impossible and highly dangerous undertaking. Indeed, Bennett had already foreseen the danger and the light was fading. They had to make it before dark or an almost certain fatal crash would follow, only miles from a destination they had worked so fervently and for so long to reach.

"Sir, I'm sure that the last batch of islands we passed to the west was East Timor, it can't be far."

"It isn't!" Fitzsimmons suddenly shouted leaning forward in his seat. "There."

Pointing ahead, an indistinct shape that Bennett had thought to be nothing more than haze, resolved itself into the unmistakable form of land. As they approached the light continued to fade, and the early signs of despair began to show on all their faces. Then Fitzsimmons saw water beyond the land. It was another island they had seen. It was all over. The three men looked at each other knowing now that it was only a matter of time. Suddenly, looking out ahead Quinn began to laugh. Bennett and Fitzsimmons turned and looked at him in bewildered alarm. Then, relishing the moment, Quinn stopped laughing and grinning said.

"Look sir, there's land beyond. That is an island, but it's Melville Island, not twenty miles beyond that island, is Darwin!"

With a huge collective sigh of relief, the three squinted out ahead. They had a chance. "Mr Quinn, take control of the radio and go through every channel calling for help, get me in contact with that airfield."

"Yes, sir," Quinn answered, a huge smile on his face, and snatched up the headphones. "And warn the cabin, tell them to prepare."

"Yes, sir." He disappeared momentarily and then returned. Moore came with him. Quinn began transmitting.

"Darwin airfield, Darwin airfield, mayday, mayday, this is Royal Air Force Dakota do you read? Over." Moore smiled at Bennett. "We made it."

"Not yet we haven't," Bennett said coldly. "Are the combustibles ready?" Moore grinned.

"We're ready, don't worry."

"Darwin airfield, Darwin airfield, mayday, mayday, this is Royal Air Force Dakota do you read? Over." Flicking through the channels, Quinn repeated the call over and over until finally a cracked reply came. The accent was unmistakable.

"Royal Air Force Dakota, this is Darwin receiving, state your emergency." Quinn assumed a look of deathly calm.

"Darwin airfield, this is Royal Air Force Dakota we have a fire onboard, approaching from the north over Melville Island and need to get wheels on the deck as soon as possible."

"Royal Air Force Dakota, Darwin, come on down we will have the Fire department ready."

"There it is, sir," Fitzsimmons said trying to hide his elation and pointing dead ahead.

"Gear down," Bennett replied. Then he turned to Quinn. "That was an exemplary piece of navigation, Mr Quinn, I thank you."

"My pleasure, sir." In near darkness the Dakota lined up for its final approach and Bennett nodded to Quinn who turned and shouted into the cabin. "Light her up!" Sharpe, once again looking serious and stood only feet behind Quinn nodded, and knelt down, lighting a ready fuse. Within seconds the cabin filled with smoke and Morgan opened the rear door as Quinn reached up and jettisoned the hatch leading out the roof of the cockpit. Even as he did so the wheels touched the runway and the aircraft began to slow. Bennett and Fitzsimmons released their belts.

"Now," Bennett shouted.

Now Morgan lit another fuse and almost immediately a flame burst from one, then another, then another location in the cabin. Having lit the fuse, Morgan and the others quickly moved to the rear doors and, shoving out a number of bundles, boxes and crates, followed them out the door falling hard on the tarmac and rolling. Eventually the aircraft came to a halt and Bennett, Quinn, and Fitzsimmons began jumping up and out the hatch in the cockpit roof. Quinn was first out holding a bundle of rope and threw it down to the ground. One by one they descended the rope and ran to distance themselves from the burning aircraft. With only seconds to spare everybody was clear just as the flames reached the cunningly hidden stash of shells. The aircraft erupted in a huge explosion and scattered parts all around the field. What was left of the fuel ignited as well and a mushroom cloud of thick black smoke rolled into the air. The newly arrived fire crews had no hope of making any headway and knew it, so hung back and watched as the remains of the aircraft collapsed and was engulfed.

"I really hope there's nobody still in there?" a fireman said as he approached Bennett.

"There isn't," Bennett replied bluntly.

"Where you boys come from?" Bennett turned on the man.

"I need my men looked after and their baggage with them. Nobody is to touch it except my men, understood? Can you take me to whoever is in charge here?"

The fireman smiled. "Sure mate. Follow me."

Bennett and Moore followed him and as they walked toward the tower the fireman shouted to his men. "Put it out, Jim take these boys to the canteen make sure their baggage goes with them."

It wasn't far and when they reached the tower a man in his middle fifties stepped out. "Blimey gents, that looked like a close-run thing, did you all get out OK?"

"They did," the fireman replied.

"Squadron Leader Bennett." Holding out his hand. Smiling the man stepped forward and shook Bennett's hand warmly.

"Julius, Julius Tucker, Temporary Director of Operations."

"Is there somewhere we could talk in private?"

"Of course, sir, follow me."

Turning to the fireman he said, "Thank you, Mr Clay." Tucker led them away from the tower and into a large building. They walked through and into an office.

"Do please have a seat, gentlemen." Bennett and Moore sat down on some easy chairs. "Sir," Bennett said, "What I'm about to tell you must remain strictly between us is that completely understood?"

"You may rely on it, sir," Tucker said and assumed an air of calm interest. "A few weeks ago, a military cargo ship travelling north from New Zealand got into trouble in a storm and having suffered damage landed at Port Moresby for repairs. That ship was carrying certain items that I will not trouble you by describing but suffice to say, they are critically important to certain power struggles currently ensuing north of here. Far from wishing these items taken north, my orders are to get these items as far away as possible, England, and furthermore to do it in absolute secrecy. It was intended that we fly to Borneo and from there get a ship that was set to leave exactly on a set schedule, a schedule we now have no hope of making, and get them home. So, I am now in a difficult position. I cannot fly, I cannot call for help, I cannot divert any operation that in so doing would alert people that we do not want alerted, that something is afoot. Therefore, I have no choice but to get myself, my men and my cargo back home by our own means. What I need from you, sir, is transport to the nearest place where we may find a ship to take us back to England with the greatest expedition. Can you help us? And most importantly, can you help us in a way that will arouse no suspicion whatsoever?"

"I can sir, we fly regularly to Perth, and I can have you and your men on a flight there first thing tomorrow morning. I have a DC6 that was going anyway and there are many spaces still remaining. Once there you should easily be able to find a ship bound for England. But if I were you, sir, I would start by getting out of your uniforms. They alone will raise interest, even if not suspicion." Hiding his total lack of knowledge as to what a DC6 was, Bennett smiled and answered, "Thank you, sir, I am indebted to you."

"Not at all."

That night lying in my bed I lay thinking over all the things I had learnt that day. It was incredible, that morning my father had been a man who led a squadron to a country unintentionally and turned the situation around and was assisting in the building and repair of that country and the training of the men that would protect it. That night as I lay there the story had become a great deal more complex. Not only that, but it had instilled in me a great fear. Was my father's crash an accident? I had to find out.

We had all sat round the table for hours that day. We had not moved except whilst Mother had prepared lunch. We had not moved at all for dinner. Mother had listened, occasionally putting in a comment but for the most part trying to busy herself around the house. It was clear she was finding that the time she had been around was painful to say the least. Finally, growing tired and clearly worn out from the experience, Earl had gone to bed and with that hint, Chungjwa and Hector left. Hector was due to leave the next day, but I couldn't help but think that I had much left to learn. Had their plan worked? What did my father think of what had happened? I glanced over to my desk where the journal lay. "No," I told myself. "Rest. Remember what you have learned and have a fresh head to learn more tomorrow."

After tossing and turning for a long time, I realised I just couldn't do it. I rose, switched on the light and sat at my desk opening the journal. Flicking through the pages I returned to the page I had looked up when we had been talking earlier. My father had written a lot that day. After the routine entries of aircraft and personnel involved it continued:

We are now involved in a desperate venture, within a desperate venture and we have lost another two! Hermann Metzger was one of the finest pilots I have ever seen. The tragedy of it, is that he always seemed to fight for the wrong side. The last time it was down to a genial maniac. This time, well, though I did not bring him into this venture, I may well have kept him in it. One thing that is indisputable however, is that had it not been for him, we would all be at the bottom of the Yellow Sea right now. It should have been me. Much the same can be said for George Kilmartin, a good pilot, an honest and god-fearing man, who did all he could till the last. I do declare I nearly broke down as we dropped him into the sea. For such a fine man to meet such an end. If we get out of this, how can I ever live with myself? These men trusted me to save them, I failed.

We are now well away from Korea, having sighted no allied aircraft which I am eternally grateful for. If our ruse of NV951 had not worked, we could not possibly have survived another attack. Within the next few hours we should be in sight of the Philippine islands and from there, as long as our fuel calculations are correct, we should make Darwin. After that phase two of the plan begins. The worst thing about our current position is that we don't know if anybody knows of it. Haw far has Radar progressed in recent years? Are we being tracked? If we reach Darwin we will almost certainly have to wait until tomorrow before we can move any further, and in that time, if we are being followed, it will all be up.

I'm pretty sure I read more than I should have, I also remember flicking back to see what else had happened, but at some point, I stopped being able to concentrate as I drifted in and out of sleep and shortly after, the journal fell to the floor.

Chapter 12

The Last Post

The next morning, I found Earl still lying in his bed, leaning back on the head board, a peaceful look on his face. But quite gone from this world, a stapled few sheets in his hand. Trying to hold back the tears and knowing Mother would soon be awake I ran for all I was worth to Peaslake. It was very early and the inn doors were locked. I banged like mad until a very angry landlord came to the door.

"For God's sake…." he began. But seeing tears streaming he quickly calmed. "What is it?"

"I must fetch Mr Sharpe, something terrible has happened."

Bursting in to Hector's room I found him asleep in bed but he shot to his feet in an instant and, suddenly realising who it was, looked through blinking eyes. "William?" There was a definite look of anger on his face.

"Come quickly," I said, trying to control the emotion in my voice. "It's Earl." Sharpe's face turned pail and without a word he was throwing on clothes.

In Earl's room, Hector sat on the bed beside him and sighed deeply. In a barely audible mutter he said, "Oh Earl, my friend." The remainder of that day saw much tears and heartbreak. Hector had decided to extend his stay and by the late morning Chungjwa had appeared. When Earl's body was taken away in an ambulance, Hector and Chungjwa were stood side by side at the gate and, as the ambulance pulled out, stood ramrod straight at the unmistakable position of attention. The scene was just too much for me and I went to my room and cried like my heart would break. It was mid-afternoon before rational thought began to return and with it, thoughts of my fathers' death. I had to find out what had happened. I was wasting time, and there was nothing I could do for Earl. There was something I could do for myself though. I went downstairs and found Hector, Chungjwa and Mother sat round the kitchen table. Mother had clearly been crying. Rising to her feet as I came in she asked, "William, do you want a cup of tea? I wanted to talk to you about the paper Earl had."

"Thank you no, I'm going out for a bit."

"Oh, ah, OK."

Thinking if I stayed that it all might be too much I quickly left. Heading for Peaslake once more, I walked past the war memorial and then out of Peaslake again on another road. Just down the road several driveways climbed a steep embankment and one of these I walked up and knocked on the door. As I knew he would be, my friend Tom was first to the door.

"Hi, Will."

"Hi, Tom, could I speak to your father?"

"Dad. Um, yeah, come in."

Tom's father was a police officer at the local station and I knew he had helped during my father's accident. Tom took me through to the lounge where his father was reading a paper. He looked up and smiled.

"Hello William, how are you?"

Awkwardly I answered, "Not all that good I'm afraid, Mr Fuller."

"Oh?"

"Earl died last night."

The paper dropped and a look of surprise and hurt crossed his face. "Oh, I am sorry to hear that, William, truly sorry, he was a good man."

"I appreciate that, Mr Fuller, but I have come for another reason."

"Oh, you have, have you?"

"I want to know about my father's crash."

He said nothing so I continued.

"I have found some things out, sir." He did not move.

"Things that make me think that my father was not happy." It sounded weak and I knew it. "Things that make me think that maybe my father's accident... might not have been an accident."

"Oh, don't be daft Will, nobody would hurt your father." Tom laughed.

"Tom, your mother wants a hand moving some boxes in the garden why don't you go and give her a hand."

"But Dad," Tom protested.

"Now Tom." Tom looked downcast but walked out. His father stared straight at me.

"William I'm not able..." He began.

"Sir, I just want to know what happened." I put on my most pleading look. "Please, sir."

"Your father was a man who liked speed. Heaven knows how many times I have spoken to him about it. He was occasionally reckless…"

"Sir," I cut in, but he cut me off as if I hadn't spoken.

"But he was a good driver, he knew the roads like the back of his hand, and the day was fine, cold yes, but fine. Yet he crashed into a bridge on a straight road."

There was a long pause as this sank in.

"William, I don't know what happened, truly I don't. All I do know is that at that speed, the end would have been very quick. Take comfort from that. That, and the sure knowledge that regardless of what he might have done, he loved you very much." So that was it. Mr Fuller knew what I was thinking, he might have tried to soften the blow, he might not have known for sure. But he certainly suspected.

"Thank you, Mr Fuller."

"William, you've had a hard time lately. But all things mend with time. Keep your chin up."

"I will, Mr Fuller, thank you."

As I walked back home I thought about what he had said. He was wrong, of course. My journey over recent days had shown me, if nothing else, that time may heal a lot… but it did not heal all. Some scars are just too deep, I guess. My father may not have been killed in battle, but as far as I could see, the battle had almost certainly killed him. I wondered if Mother knew. She probably suspected, but didn't want to believe it. I didn't blame her. I somehow felt I should blame my father. Did I not know the full story, I probably would have. But now? Well, I couldn't blame him now, he had been through hell, not once, not twice, but so many times. He never forgot what had happened, he probably didn't want to. A self-imposed punishment for what he saw as being all his fault. I could have been wrong, of course, but I thought not. My mind cast back, and my eyes fell on the side pocket of my sachel, I had picked it up when I left hoping it might be able to divert me from the present. I opened the side pocket and drew out the letter I had found turning it over in my fingers. To hell with it I though and folded it open. No date, no location or stamp. It had been folded twice and as it opened I realised with a thrill that it was a letter from my father to his father.

Dear Father

Weep you might when you hear of my many adventures. It would remind you of our treasure hunts when I was a boy. My whistles and tops are now victories and lives saved... and taken. It seems odd that in a place with so much death, I have never felt so alive. I know in time of war my efforts must seem small, even insignificant but I remain diligent and resolute in my belief in the necessity of our cause.

No one person or people can claim the world and I would and will exact my best efforts to prevent this. My convictions and beliefs guard and protect me from a fate I know must come. Father, I know I have been a great disappointment. In defence of the indefensible my failures were failures I was led to with the best of intentions, not actions bent on hurting you. I did all I could, but it was not enough.

I long for the chance to be back on that pedestal on which you so proudly once placed me. Perhaps here I can make you proud again. I am sorry and grateful and longing for home, and rest.

I am in great need of rest.

I will write again when I can.

My love to you and mother

Your devoted son

Allan

I stood thunderstruck and heartbroken. Tears welled and fell. I had no idea when he had written it, but it didn't matter. The letter made my father human again, and all the thoughts of loss of both him and Earl flooded back. It was too much.

When I got home I found everybody where I had left them. Chungjwa stood up as I walked in. He bowed as he so often did, then took the few steps and said in a whisper, "We can not bring back the people we have lost. But we can remember them. But to remember them, we must know their story. Do you wish to continue?" Once more brushing a tear aside I forced a smile.

"Yes."

He nodded and gestured to a chair. Hector smiled.

"I intend to stay a while, and with Earl… Well… not here. I guess it falls to me to continue your father's story." There was a pause and as if cleansing himself he let out sharp sigh. And smiled. "And this includes discussing this." He held up the papers Earl had been holding when he died.

"What are they?" Chungjwa answered for him.

"Notes."

At my questioning look he went on.

"Earl was an old man. He could not remember everything that happened, so he had written notes to remind himself. What is written he spoke to you of but at the end he writes things he wanted to give you that he never got the chance to."

"What things?"

"We don't know, we only know where they are." Handing me the papers they all looked on. I speed read the last sheet, recognising much of what had been written, but half way down the last page a line had been drawn across the page and beneath it was the words: 'Give him the chest, explain contents.'

I looked up.

"My father's chest?"

"Yes," Mother answered.

"Where is it?"

"In the loft," Mother said. "But Earl clearly intended to finish the story first."

I sat down at the table looking at them all and trying to concentrate.

"I suppose we had better do that then." I said resignedly.

Hector, as if waiting for his cue began.

"Well, having made it to Darwin, we were stuck there for the night. Mr Tucker had arranged to have a side building that had some beds in it given to us for the night. We shifted in all the baggage and boxes and took it in turns sleeping and keeping watch. You see, we didn't know if we had been followed, tracked, we had no idea. If we were, and our location was known then that night would be the time when our pursuers caught up. But they never did. The night was as quiet as a mill pond. The next morning, at first light, Tucker knocked on the door and told us to load everything we wanted to go with us into this big brute of an aircraft sat on a hardstand nearby. About one hour after that, we had stowed everything onto the DC6 but we had some time to kill, so your father suggested we went for a walk round the field. We had walked some distance from the buildings when your father stopped and turned on us.

The early morning sun shone down on the little group on the edge of the field. Only Aircraftsman Adaway was absent. He had stayed with the aircraft to keep an eye on the luggage. They were all now dressed in civilian clothes, some helpfully provided by Julius Tucker.

'Gentlemen, your attention please.' The men gathered round in a half circle with Bennett and Fitzsimmons in the centre.

'Gentlemen, I hope you slept well, and are up for a new day. Before we leave I have a few things to say.' He had their attention and they looked on expectantly. Bennett looked at them one at a time, his face grave. Then he allowed a half smile. 'We have been through a lot, too much. We have lost friends, people we care for, and will miss. But now it is over and I believe I owe you an explanation as to why we suddenly left so precipitately.

'As you all know, we shot down an American aircraft in our last days at Kangaroo and captured the crew. From them we were able to satisfy ourselves that we had been lied to the entire time we had been in Korea. Those papers that they got for us, were fake. After '45, the world had been at peace as we thought but the world had continued as it had before the war, not as we were told. The Americans have done nothing wrong in that respect. Korea had been divided. The north under communist rule, the south under allied rule. It was not the Americans that invaded Korea, it was the communists who invaded the south and we had been tricked into helping the wrong side. Wanting to be sure, I asked Chungjwa to make discreet enquiries and we found it to be true. I'm very sorry to say he found out something else as well. I regret to tell you that the men who left when we first arrived in Korea, and were told they would be given safe passage home… were murdered as soon as they had left.'

Muttering broke out and anger was plane to see in the faces of all. Bennett held up a hand.

'Gentlemen it is for this reason that I deemed it necessary to leave immediately. But now we are free of the country I cannot help but realise that none of this would have even begun had it not been for decisions I had made, and the responsibility I bear for them you may believe is grievously difficult to bear. I truly am… deeply sorry.' Even as he said it, his voice quivered, his eyes filled and tears began to run.

Shocked by the news, and obviously sympathetic to the hurting figure in front of them nobody seemed able to say anything. Finally, Moore spoke, addressing them all.

'I know I speak for the officers when I say that we made our own decisions to stay. Those decisions being based on information that was false and therefore I hold no man responsible for them, except those that told the lies.'

Morgan stepped forward. 'You speak for me also.'

Then, one by one. Each man spoke, 'And I.' Visibly relieved, Bennett took a deep breath and tried to compose himself.

'Gentlemen, in a short time, we will embark on that aircraft.' He pointed at the DC6 in the distance. 'And when we land in Perth I will secure us a ship home. However, I am done making decisions for you, this is your choice. I want to make clear that you are no longer under my command, or that of the other officers. We are no longer a military unit. We are a group, a group destined for wherever you, as individuals wish to go.'

'Where are you going to go, sir?' Squires asked.

'I intend to return to England and I will be happy to take you with me. But if you wish to stay in Australia then I wish you all the very best... And it's Allan now, lads.'

There were smiles all around.

'Come on then, gentlemen, I'm headed home.'

The group slowly made their way back to the hardstand and one by one, all clearly engrossed in their own thoughts, they boarded. The DC6 was half cargo plane, half passenger, and there were two couples sat down already and a man dressed smartly and reading a book. Exchanging pleasant smiles as they passed them, they all took seats as far back as they could, next to the door that led through to the cargo area.

Sitting down in his seat Sharpe looked at Quinn and grinned. 'Bit more comfortable than the last flight.'

Quinn grinned back.

'In more ways than one.'

As the DC6 gained speed down the runway, Bennett, Moore, Fitzsimmons and Chungjwa were sat together. Bennett turned to Moore who was staring all around them.

'What is it, Earl?'

'Well,' Earl said with a smile. 'It would seem that aviation has progressed somewhat since '45.'

Bennett initially gave a small smile but said nothing. Then a shadow crossed his face and he looked so stricken that Earl was about to ask him what was wrong but before he spoke Bennett at last spoke. "We lost good men discovering that."

Well into the flight Fitzsimmons turned to Bennett.

'Sir…'

'Allan,' Bennett corrected him. Fitzsimmons smiled sheepishly.

'Allan, I've been thinking and, well I'm not going back to England. I'm going to stay in Perth.'

Bennett looked at him questioningly.

'I don't think of England as home anymore, I have no family left and Australia well, less rain. More opportunity.'

Bennett chuckled in a way none of them had heard for some time.

'OK, John, of course. What will you do?'

'Oh, I don't know, I'm sure there is use for a pilot somewhere out here.'

'I'm sure there is.' Bennett agreed. Chungjwa smiled and said.

'Australia too hot for me, I going to England. But it will be hard I think. I not like you, I have no money.' Earl cut in.

'You can come with me, I could use a hand.'

'With what?' Bennett asked.

'I'm old enough to know when I've had enough of my chosen road in life. I'm going to retire, become a gardener.'

Bennett let out a laugh, so natural and so long that Fitzsimmons and Chungjwa joined in. Quinn, Sharpe and Gerard turned in astonishment at their complete senior officer core laughing like children. The laughter subsided and Bennett wiped away a tear.

'You're not serious?'

'I am,' Moore answered stubbornly. 'I've often thought about it but I figured the money would be bad, but that's not quite such a worry now, is it? If you want to join me we can make a business of it. Military Officer to earth shoveler, your career's progressing my friend.'

Chungjwa laughed again.

'Our situation may be even better than you think,' Bennett said mysteriously.

'Oh?' Fitzsimmons said, 'and how is that?'

'Well, before we left I relieved the station pay and cash chest of its contents, that's all.' And he grinned again. They all laughed again. The strain and fear was lifting and they were showing hints of returning to the people they had once been.

"That was the last flight I ever went on, would you believe it? Hector said.

"Mine too," Chungjwa added.

"Have you never been back?" I asked carefully.

"I probably couldn't. They'd arrest me as soon as I got there, whichever side of the lines I landed on, and anyway, it's been nearly twenty years. My life is here, I love this country, this place."

"So, what happened when you landed?"

Hector took up the story.

"Well that man from the Darwin airfield had sent a note to the authorities, all official and such, stating that we were to be taken to Perth port as soon as we landed, explaining the reason that none of us had passports and I believe it said we were officers on a mission of importance. Whatever, it worked and when we got to the port we had no problems finding a ship headed home. Fitzsimmons, Gerard and four of the others had decided to stay in Australia and so your father, Chungjwa, Earl, myself, Mr Quinn, Morgan and Squires all boarded a cargo ship that had agreed to take us and it was due to leave the next day. So there we stayed, not wanting to meet anybody who might ask questions, and the next day the ship steamed out of port and our time in Australia was done."

"Hold on a second," I said as a thought struck me. I left the room, went upstairs and grabbed my father's journal then returned to the kitchen. Sitting down I opened it and turned to the relevant page. The others looked on as I read:

4th October 1950

We are now on our way to Perth. Phase two worked admirably, despite my doubts. Mr Fitzsimmons and some of the NCO's have decided to stay here in Australia and I don't blame them. It does seem a truly beautiful place but I must get home. I yearn to see England again. I want to put all this behind me but I fear I may never shake the sense of responsibility I feel for the death of so many good men, nor the shame of being gulled into supporting a regime that has turned out to be no better than the regime I spend a world war trying to bring down. I find myself wondering if those people I killed over Africa, France and Germany were the same as me. Tricked into fighting for something they believed was right because they had been lied to the whole time. Maybe the creation and maintenance of war is reliant solely on a pack of lying politicians stringing a convincing yarn. And in the end, whether a side wins or loses it doesn't really matter, because the only people who died were the insignificant ones, while the real power at the top remain safe in their beds with their bank accounts full. I pray I am wrong.

Realising I was keeping the others waiting, I snapped out of it.

"I'm sorry, I just wanted to keep up." Hector looked at me with sudden hostility.

"Don't you believe me?"

Before I had time to answer Chungjwa, teeth grinding, and glaring at Hector in the first show of emotion I had ever seen from him spat,

"Don't be a damn fool, Sharpe! William is learning his father's story. We are here to help but the story must come from his father himself as much, if not more, than us! This book," he placed his hand on the journal, "is the only thing that remains of Mr Bennett. Nobody has more right to read it whenever he damn well pleases as Master William does, so hold your damn tongue!"

Hector's face melted.

"I apologise. Thoughtless of me."

I looked at him and smiled.

"That's alright. Do go on."

Hector sighed, sat back in his chair and continued.

"Well, I'd seen bloody canal barges that were faster but at least we were on our way. Weeks later, when we were cruising up the English Channel the ship steamed close to shore near Dartmouth and we all disembarked using one of their escape launches."

"Escape launches!" I asked, amazed.

"Yep, the crew rowed us in, baggage and all, landed us on this huge beach in darkness right beside some little village called Strete. If I remember right it was only about five o'clock in the afternoon." He chuckled. "I never knew that silence cost so much."

"How do you mean?"

"I mean, we paid the beggars to keep their damn mouths shut. Mind you, even if they hadn't, they had no idea who we were, but anyway. Guess what we did first thing?"

"What?"

Hector was laughing as he answered, "Went and had a beer."

Chungjwa cut in. "You went for the beer, I went for the fire! I was so cold."

"Oh yes," Hector said, clearly suddenly remembering. "It was freezing, so cold you would not believe. Mind you, it was December by then. Anyway, we sat round the fire and made enquiries as to where we could stay that night. But there was nowhere available so we paid some guy to take us to Dartmouth in his dodgy old truck and stayed in a hotel there. I remember Earl was so excited as it had been decades since he had been back in his home county. But he didn't have any family or home there anymore.

"Anyway, it had to end of course, and next morning we all went for a walk down the harbour and followed the estuary until there was nobody around."

Bennett stood as he had done in Australia with the few men remaining standing round.

'So, chaps, the time has come I think for us to go our separate ways. I don't know if we will see each other again, but I do wish you all well.'

Opening a bag he had been carrying he handed out a bundle for each of them.

'When we left Kangaroo, I took all the money in the pay chests and the base safe. I know you are all wealthy men now but this is what I took, divided up. It is also the pay of those friends we have left behind in Korea. There is nobody else I can give it to, and I know they would want it this way. It's all equal, I promise, no rank or service difference. I gave the others we left in Australia the same.'"

One by one Bennett approached every man and shook each warmly by the hand speaking quietly to each. Finally, he stepped back.

'Good luck gentlemen.'

A silence fell over them all and after a brief pause Bennett gave them all a salute a parade ground would have been proud of. It was just as smartly returned and then the group broke up and the days of the Devil's Squadron were well and truly over. Only Bennett, Moore and Chungjwa remained and they walked around the town together talking, and to give the others time to get their things out of the hotel they went to lunch near the dock. Sat at the table plans were discussed and memories re-visited. That afternoon, having decided to stay in Dartmouth a little longer, but deciding to shift location closer to the waterfront and a larger hotel, they shifted their gear once again and by that night were happily sat in the bar having dinner.

"And guess who they met there?" It was Mother. I stared at her in amazement. It was the first time she had spoken for some time and the memory of that far away place and time even brought a small smile.

"You?"

"Oh yes, I was working behind the bar. Later that night you," she said, looking at Chungjwa, "went to bed and your father was still sat there. I was finishing work and he bought me a drink, and well, I guess the rest is history." She sighed. "Twenty years," She said wistfully. Her eyes welled up and she looked at me with begging sympathy. "I know he was a hard man to understand. But I've never seen him so happy as the day you were born. He had an awkward way of showing it, but he loved you very much." Tears began to run slowly down her now red cheeks. "He could never forgive himself for what happened after the war. He hated himself for it, and he blamed himself entirely for the people he lost in Korea."

Chungjwa rose.

"I make a cup of tea for you," he said, looking on in sympathy at my mother and gave a gentle smile. "You English believe all problems solved by tea." Mother smiled and wiped her tears.

"I have to say, William," Hector continued. "There is not much else I can tell you. As a unit it was over, we survived, we went our separate ways. Many took on new names, new identities, I never did figure out how your father got away with keeping his name."

"A friend," Mother suddenly put in. Both me and Hector looked at her questioningly. She went on. "Your father had a friend from his days in Africa who by the time we came to Surrey in '52 was very high in the RAF. I believe your father approached him and said he had been a prisoner in Korea until 1950, having crashed on the way to Japan. It was hushed up at your father's request and would you believe it, the RAF even gave him the back pay for five years captivity. But nothing was said publicly or privately. In the end it meant that we could live here with your father's reputation intact. But in many ways, this made him worse as he felt that he had betrayed trust as well as his country. About three years ago I thought he was finally improving but then the nightmares came back and he was lost to me again."

Tears rolled again and right on cue, Chungjwa placed a cup of tea in front of her. "Thank you so much," she said through her tears. "We'll never know what happened the day your father died, but I hope he found peace at last."

She knows, I thought with a stab of anguish, she knows.

I thought Mother had finished but then she spoke again. "All this is why you have never met my parents, or your fathers'. They knew of what had happened, and although I knew they would say nothing, they never forgave your father."

Biting back the temptation to pass judgement on my grandparents, I just said. "So, I guess we had better find that chest then?"

"I'll show you where it is," Mother said.

In a very few short minutes the chest I had once seen in my father's office rested on the floor in the kitchen. It was smaller than I remembered it but the same in appearance. Mother opened a drawer and produced a set of keys. Bending to the locks she inserted the keys one after another and opened it.

"God," Mother exclaimed, for the first thing that caught the eye was a service revolver and a box of bullets. "He never told me he had that!" Neatly folded in one side of the chest from bottom to top were my father's uniforms. Straight away I noticed working, full dress, and flying uniforms. In the remaining third of the chest, lying on top of various items, was my father's uniform cap, and flying hat. The dried-out leather cracking with time. I picked them up. At once I spotted something I had been looking for. A small leather-bound box. When I opened the lid, sure enough, inside were medals. Eight medals stared up at me many with bars. I knew them all, save one. With no ribbon, it was a large series of stars laid one over the other, all a dull silver and in the centre, surrounded by blue and red enamel was a final small gold star. I picked it up. Chungjwa stepped forward and gently took it from me. Rubbing it with his thumb he looked down at it lovingly.

"I never thought he kept it," he said softly.

"What is it?" I asked.

"That's the gong the Koreans gave him," Hector added. I took it back and placed it on top of the others, then closed the box and put it on the kitchen table. Hector bent down and picked up the revolver but, like a cat, my mother pounced and snatched it out of his hand.

"Oh no you don't," she said, fixing Hector with an unmoving stare, "that's going straight into a deep hole in the garden!" Feeling a pang of disappointment at the thought I turned my attention back to the chest. There were some tankards, a plaque with an RAF Squadron crest. Then my eye caught a watch. The glass was smashed and the whole thing had evidently been burnt for long enough that the strap was very delicate, and the case blackened.

I picked it out and turned it over in my hands. My mother answered the unspoken question. "Your uncle Tom's," she said softly.

Very gently I placed it back. Then I noticed a strange item. It was a block of dark wood about eight by six inches, and drilled into it was a shell casing from the end of which protruded three more fanned out and then another three at the end of them. This made the object a similar shape to a pitchfork. I picked it up and rotated in in my hand. On the front of the block, which had been finely polished, was a plaque. Before I had time to read, Hector's knowing chuckle cut in. Rolling my eyes so he couldn't see I sighed and turned.

"Go on then, what on earth is this?"

"What do you think? 'The Devil's Squadron', that's what we were called, every devil needs a fork so…"

I stared at it again.

"We made it to put behind the bar. I thought it was probably still there but here it is."

Standing it to one side, I returned to the chest once again. Pulling out a small bundle of thick cloth I spread it out. It was a small triangular flag, what in the old days had been called a pennant. Hector spoke again.

"That's the flag they gave the squadron at the same time as your father got his gong."

Finally, there were a set of large books. Opening the first I realised they were albums. Turning the pages, I saw photograph after photograph. What a treasure. I placed the albums on the kitchen table and only then noticed the camera that had presumably taken the photos, sat in the bottom of the chest. The words 'Kodak 35' stood out in the centre.

"Blimey" I exclaimed. "So this is what Earl wanted to show me."

"Your father never even let me open this," Mother added. The box was taken into the lounge and put in a corner and I took the albums and medals up to my room.

In the days that followed we buried Earl beside my father in the little graveyard on the hill. The doctors found that he had suffered a blood clot, which apparently was not unusual for people of Earl's age that had been inactive for lengths of time. Personally though, I couldn't help but feel that Earl had finally got something off his chest he had carried for so long, and how he finally felt his work was done. Hector returned to his home in Yorkshire and I never heard from him again. In 1975 I joined the Royal Air Force and after my time at Cranwell went on to fly first the Lightning, and then the Tornado, ending up in Desert Storm. After a long period of consideration, I found my grandparents, who I learned had been desperate to meet me. But our first meeting I think was not what they had hoped it would be. I berated them for their lack of understanding of my father and for failing to see his life for what it had really been. We remained in contact but I struggled to understand how they could have been so naïve in the way they had treated us and the connection never really formed.

Chungjwa became a regular visitor and close friend of both myself, and my mother until his death in 1992, having never once returned to his home country. Upon his death, a gentleman turned up at my mother's home saying that Chungjwa had left both his home and all his money to us. We buried him with my father and Earl, as his will had requested. My mother passed away only a year later. I married of course, and had two children. I never told them of what I had learned about my father except his World War Two life, and even that I limited. I felt it was a story I, and I alone needed to know. I guess I worried that they might not understand.

After a long career in the RAF, I had on many occasions led men into combat and for a short period commanded a squadron and it was only really then that I began to get a true sense of what my father must have felt like after what had happened. Bad enough to lead men into battle and lose them. So much worse under the circumstances my father found himself in. His World War Two service would have already been enough to severely affect him, but to pile what happened in Korea on top of that would have been a crippling blow to the toughest of men.

In 1994, I sold my mother's home in the valley. I had long gone already of course and lived in Kent, but though I loved Peaslake and my beloved forest, I had lost too much there. I went back from time to time and finally one day in about 1997, I made up my mind as to what to do with my father's journal. Late one summer's evening I drove up from Kent, parked in the centre of Peaslake next to the inn, and when it was almost completely dark I crept up to the group of four headstones I knew so well. Taking out a collapsible shovel I buried it between the graves of Earl and my father.

I remember standing there as I had so many times before thinking about the days so many years ago when I had learned of my father's story and that of his men. They were probably all gone now, and many of their names had faded from my memory. Now the record of them was gone too, almost like it had never happened.

Author's Note

I have to confess that when I first began researching history and getting involved in solving historical mysteries, I had no time for fiction. The true stories made for exciting reading enough, and you can't research fiction. Or so I thought at the time.

However much later on, I read Len Deighton's 'Bomber' and even as a child I loved the stories of Bernard Cornwell's 'Sharpe' and CS Forester's 'Hornblower' and finally, only a few years back, Julian Stockwin's 'Kydd', and I began to realise that whilst these don't tell factual stories, they are often at least partially based on true stories, and more than that, if they are well researched they can give you a real insight into life in the time period the book is based in. Now I for one am a bit tunnel visioned, and can't possibly understand why anybody could ever not be interested in history. I have often quoted round the dinner table as my exasperated friends and family look on at the telling of yet another historical tale, the words. 'Those who do not study history are condemned to learn its lessons again.' My interpretation and tweaking of the words of the Spanish philosopher George Santayana who actually said, 'Those who can't remember the past are condemned to repeat it.' This was later picked up by Winston Churchill by which time it had become, 'Those who fail to learn from history are doomed to repeat it.'

Anyway, novels about historical events, whilst they could hardly be called research, do at the very least, increase interest in a historical period amongst those who otherwise would not show any interest at all, and I love that idea. Then it was one night round such a dinner table that a friend asked me, "Could old propeller planes go up against jets and stand a chance?" As the rest rolled their eyes and looked witheringly at my friend at having opened the flood gates to yet another barrage of history, his simple question set me thinking. Now, for the most part, the answer would be no but in some cases, with certain aircraft in the transitional period between props and jets between 1944 and 1955, I found myself thinking that not only would the prop aircraft have a chance, but possibly even a better chance than if they had gone up against other prop aircraft. From there I began tests on flight simulators, trawled through records of Messerschmitt 262's going up against prop fighters, and Yaks going up against the US in Korea. Finally, from the results of that research the seeds were sown for the righting of this, my first novel.

Although the idea of an underground airbase may seem absurd, they did exist in large numbers, during and after the Second World War and indeed, continue to exist. Whenever a modern war has been fought with one side in control of the skies, the other has gone underground to disguise and hide things they didn't want attacked. This tactic was pioneered by the Germans hiding their V2 rocket development facility, and at about the same time by the Japanese hiding airbases just like in this book, and yes, many of these were later used by the Soviets and North Koreans and even today there are some still with MiG 17's sitting dusty and unused in long rows deep underground. Examples of this type of base are also to be found in China, India and Albania and several other countries.

The story I tell of the combat mission that killed Bennett's brother' Tom, did actually take place. An ill-considered raid led to the entire attacking force of 18 Squadron Blenheim's being shot down. Wing Commander Malcom himself was the last aircraft shot down in flames and he was awarded the Victoria Cross posthumously.

To my knowledge and according to my research, Tempest Fighters never operated outside Europe during World War Two. Probably due to the complexities of servicing and almost certainly because of their inability to fly long distance. Their engines, the twenty-four cylinder, Napier Sabre IIB, were quite simply a marvel of engineering and even today can be considered one of the most advanced aviation piston engines ever made churning out 2,400 horse power. By the end of its production in 1946, the engineers at Hawker had added another thousand to that. However, if there was one thing they were not, it was economical. Even with external fuel tanks Sabre IIB just didn't have the ability to fly for hours and hours on end, like the well-known American fighters of the time. At their most economical estimates suggest that their range was at most 809 miles with external drop tanks.

So why Hawker Tempests? Well, of all the aircraft I tested and researched, the Tempest seemed to be the one which when put against jets had the better chance. The Tempest's four 20mm cannon packed a massive punch and would do great damage to a jet in a short burst. The Tempest was a rugged aircraft and would take a burst from American aircraft of the time without too much trouble. (most American aircraft still using machine guns rather than cannon). Finally, the most obvious reason, speed. The Tempest was capable of speeds up to and including 432MPH. That puts it 145MPH slower than the F80 Shooting Star and 113MPH slower than the F9F Panther. But it gave it a better fighting chance than any other British Fighter. It should also be noted that the Messerschmitt 262 jet pilots of World War Two generally considered the Tempest their most dangerous opponent. Indeed, the Tempest was credited with several ME262 kills during the closing days of the War, and the ME262 had a 127MPH advantage over the Tempest so there is an easy comparison there.

In any event, I chose this aircraft because I love it, and this story because I love it. It may not have happened but it could have. Give the Tempests the advantage of surprise (a fighter's ultimate advantage), the ability to outturn an opponent, and superior experience to the pilots, and they could have been a match for jet fighters of the period.

I hope very much that anybody who has taken the time to read this book has enjoyed doing so. I may have spent many years as a historian but very few as an author so any comments and feedback are always welcome and valued, be it good or bad. I would also be more than happy to assist others in historical research of this period and indeed any period between 1750 to present day. If I can be of any assistance, do please feel free to contact me.

sgt_kimbell@hotmail.com

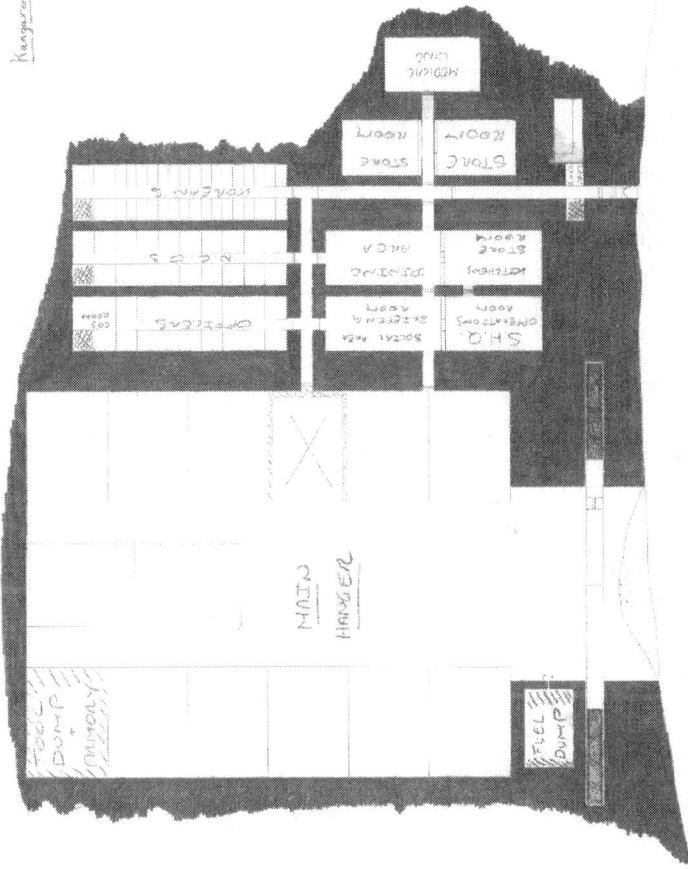

Glossary of Terms

AHQ – Air Headquarters

V2 – The V2 rocket or 'Aggregat 4' was the first ever long range guided ballistic missile. Over 3000 were produced and were responsible for the deaths of an estimated 9000 people. It had a 200 mile operational range.

CO – Commanding Officer

NCO – Non Commissioned Officer

DFC – Distinguished Flying Cross, a Military award given to pilots and aircrew of the Royal Air Force and Fleet Air Arm for acts of extreme gallantry in the face of the enemy.

DSO – Distinguished Service Order, Generally accepted as the second highest award for bravery a person can receive. The DSO can be awarded to any member of the Army, Navy or Air Force.

CMG – Companion of St Michael and St George, Awarded for distinguished service in the Colonies and Protectorates of the British Empire

DC3 – Twin engined Airliner and Military Transport aircraft developed in the 1930's by the Douglas Aircraft Company.

DC6 – Four engined transport aircraft built in 1946 originally intended as a military transport but when the war ended it was adapted to operate as a commercial airliner.

Yak – (Yakovlev) is a Russian aircraft manufacturer founded in 1934 and continues to this day. It has been responsible for the production of some of the finest propeller aircraft ever made.

Split S – An air combat manoeuvre with multiple uses. It is where an aircraft in level flight, rolls upside down and then pulls hard back on the stick diving the aircraft initially vertically down but then continuing round until the aircraft is level again facing the opposite way it was when the manoeuvre was begun.

Scramble – Aviation term used to describe the motions of getting aircraft and crew from readiness (aware that they may be called) to flight as quickly as possible.

Echelon – An Air Force formation (a way multiple aircraft fly together). In this case each aircraft is stationed diagonally behind and to the right of each other in a continuous line.

Line Astern – An Air Force formation the same as Echelon but instead of spreading out diagonally to the left or right. It is a dead straight line from the leader at the front straight back one after another

Line Abreast – An Air Force formation the same as Echelon but instead of spreading out diagonally to the left or right or behind (line Astern) it is a dead straight line from the leader sideways.

Wingover - An aerobatic manoeuvre in which an airplane makes a steep climb, followed by a vertical flat-turn (the plane turns to its side, without rolling, similar to the way a car turns). The manoeuvre ends with a short dive as the plane gently levels out, flying in the opposite direction from which the manoeuvre began.

P51 – P51 Mustang, single engined American fighter aircraft, began production in 1940 and eventually left all military service in 1984. Generally accepted as **one** of the finest fighter aircraft of all time.

Tallyho – Originally an expression beginning around 1772 in the UK coming most likely from the French 'taille haut' it began as a war cry but later became target or goal in sight. It was later adopted formally by the Air Force as a way of announcing enemy aircraft in sight.

Friendlies - Aviation term used to describe friendly aircraft.

Bandits – Aviation term used to describe enemy aircraft.

Gong – Military slang for medal.

Prop – Propeller

RVP – Rendezvous Point. A pre-arranged position where a group will meet.

RAF – Royal Air Force
RCAF – Royal Canadian Air Force
RNZAF – Royal New Zealand Air Force
RAAF – Royal Australian Air Force

USAF – United States Air Force

RAF Ranks 1945:
> **Non Commissioned Officers (NCO's):**
>> Aircraftman (AC)
>> Leading Aircraftman (LAC)
>> Corporal (Cpl)
>> Sergeant (Sgt)
>> Flight Sergeant (FS)
>> Warrant Officer 2nd Class (WO2)
>> Warrant Officer 1st Class (WO1)

> **Officers:**
>> Pilot Officer (PO)
>> Flying Officer (FO)
>> Flight Lieutenant (FL)
>> Squadron Leader (SL)
>> Wing Commander (WC)
>> Group Captain (GC)
>> Air Commodore (ACO)
>> Air Vice Marshal (AVM)
>> Air Marshal (AM)
>> Air Chief Marshal (ACM)
>> Marshal Of The Royal Air Force

35230697R00115

Printed in Poland
by Amazon Fulfillment
Poland Sp. z o.o., Wrocław